"Stay p̶u̶t̶, ̶.̶.̶.̶.̶.̶.̶.̶ said, holding out a hand to stop her.

"I can't sit down?" Danielle asked, halting her progress into his office.

His voice dropped to a low growl. "You won't be staying that long."

"I'm in no rush," she replied, proceeding to the chair in front of his desk and sitting down.

Maxwell caught her scent, that gentle, misty fragrance he'd noticed the first time he'd encountered her. He had to get her out of here. "Go harass someone else," he said.

"I'd rather fight with you."

He glanced her way sharply. A mistake. She recrossed her legs slowly. Was she doing that on *purpose?* It wasn't possible, he decided. She wasn't that cruel.

But his mouth went dry all the same, and something kicked at his chest from the inside.

He thought it might be his heart....

Dear Reader,

We've been trying to capture what Silhouette Romance means to our readers, our authors and ourselves. In canvassing some authors, I've heard wonderful words about the characteristics of a Silhouette Romance novel—innate tenderness, lively, thoughtful, fun, emotional, hopeful, satisfying, warm, sparkling, genuine and affirming.

It pleases me immensely that our writers are proud of their line and their readers! And I hope you're equally delighted with their offerings. Be sure to drop a line or visit our Web site and let us know what we're doing right—and any particular favorite topics you want to revisit.

This month we have another fantastic lineup filled with variety and strong writing. We have a new continuity—HAVING THE BOSS'S BABY! Judy Christenberry's *When the Lights Went Out...* starts off the series about a powerful executive's discovery that one woman in his office is pregnant with his child. But who could it be? Next month Elizabeth Harbison continues the series with *A Pregnant Proposal*.

Other stories for this month include Stella Bagwell's conclusion to our MAITLAND MATERNITY spin-off. Go find *The Missing Maitland*. Raye Morgan's popular office novels continue with *Working Overtime*. And popular Intimate Moments author Beverly Bird delights us with an amusing tale about *Ten Ways To Win Her Man*.

Two more emotional titles round out the month. With her writing partner, Debrah Morris wrote nearly fifteen titles for Silhouette Books as Pepper Adams. Now she's on her own with *A Girl, a Guy and a Lullaby*. And Martha Shields's dramatic stories always move me. Her *Born To Be a Dad* opens with an unusual, powerful twist and continues to a highly satisfying ending!

Enjoy these stories, and keep in touch.

Mary-Theresa Hussey

Mary-Theresa Hussey,
Senior Editor

Please address questions and book requests to:
Silhouette Reader Service
U.S.: 3010 Walden Ave., P.O. Box 1325, Buffalo, NY 14269
Canadian: P.O. Box 609, Fort Erie, Ont. L2A 5X3

Ten Ways To
Win Her Man

BEVERLY BIRD

SILHOUETTE *Romance*®

Published by Silhouette Books

America's Publisher of Contemporary Romance

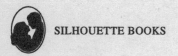

SILHOUETTE BOOKS

ISBN 0-373-19550-8

TEN WAYS TO WIN HER MAN

Books by Beverly Bird

Silhouette Romance

Ten Ways To Win Her Man #1550

Silhouette Intimate Moments

Emeralds in the Dark #3
The Fires of Winter #23
Ride the Wind #139
A Solitary Man #172
A Man Without Love #630
A Man Without a Haven #641
A Man Without a Wife #652
Undercover Cowboy #711
The Marrying Kind #732
Compromising Positions #777
†*Loving Mariah* #790
†*Marrying Jake* #802
†*Saving Susannah* #814
It Had To Be You #970
I'll Be Seeing You #1030
Out of Nowhere #1090

Silhouette Desire

The Best Reasons #190
Fool's Gold #209
All the Marbles #227
To Love a Stranger #411

*Wounded Warriors
†The Wedding Ring

BEVERLY BIRD

has lived in several places in the United States, but she is currently back where her roots began on an island in New Jersey. Her time is devoted to her family and her writing. She is the author of numerous romance novels, both contemporary and historical. Beverly loves to hear from readers. You can write to her at P.O. Box 350, Brigantine, NJ 08203.

Ten Ways To Win Her Man

1. Invest in red lace lingerie and make sure he gets a glimpse of it.

2. Give half a million dollars to his favorite charity.

3. Ditch the business suits in favor of skirts...short skirts.

4. Share his interest in sports. Let him take you out to the ball game.

5. Learn to cook. The way to a man's heart is through his stomach.

6. Spend *another* half million on the land he wants, to boggle his mind and pique his interest.

7. Be unpredictable and keep him off balance. Never be the same woman twice.

8. Wine and dine him. Bring in violinists to provide romantic music.

9. Give him long, steady come-hither looks that stop his breath.

10. And finally, when all else fails... seduce him. Or try to.

Chapter One

He entered her life at 6:22 on a Tuesday evening, and suddenly nothing was the same.

The sky outside her office window rolled with gray-black clouds at the time, uncertain if it wanted to weep, or spit late-season ice. Until it made up its mind, Danielle Dempsey Harrington chose to ignore it. She maneuvered a toy car along the miniature driveway that surrounded the elaborate model of the newest Harrington resort and she frowned.

The plans were solid, and construction would begin in twenty-six days, but now she wondered whether the grand entrance loggia should face the sea or the mountains. It was just last-minute jitters, she thought, but she fretted. The sea would be more dramatic. The mountains, dignified and majestic.

"Eeny, meeny, miney, mo," she murmured aloud. "Front or back? Beach or mountains?" And what would her project supervisor do if she changed her mind now?

"So this is how the movers and shakers get things done."

Danielle yelped at the unexpected voice behind her. She spun away from the model, and the little car sailed from her hand. It landed on her desk—amazingly, wheels down—and raced across the polished ebony surface. The man caught it in one hand just as it nosedived off the far edge. He looked down at it as it lay nestled in his palm.

"More lives saved," he murmured. "It's my calling."

Then Danielle knew who he was.

She stared at him. She couldn't breathe, she realized distractedly, then she dragged in air. Nothing—*nothing*—could have prepared her for Maxwell Padgett in the flesh, if only because that flesh was so incredible.

She'd known *of* him, of course, though she had never actually met him face-to-face before now. He was the boon of the newly elected Senator Stan Roberson's recent campaign. She thought they might be related somehow, but she couldn't remember the details. It didn't matter. Max Padgett was a force to be reckoned with on his own. She knew. His Coalition for Wildlife, Fields and Streams had been hammering at her for months now, mostly through correspondence and political maneuvering. His effort to have half a million dollars worth of Harrington land taken by eminent domain had been his most brazen bid. He'd lost, but not before costing her a small fortune in legal fees.

For that alone she should have detested him. And she had, for months. But as he stood smiling at her now, her anger and irritation siphoned out of her and left her mind blank.

"Cat got your tongue?" he asked.

Danielle opened her mouth to respond. She snapped

it shut again and looked from the car, to his face, to the car again. She needed a snappy comeback but she couldn't dredge one up because, that quickly her gaze got stuck on his hands.

They were get-things-done hands, she thought a little dazedly. Not soft, not pampered, not manicured, but with a force and presence all their own. Suddenly she imagined them on her skin—a searing image that came out of nowhere and couldn't have been more alien to her nature than pigtails and a pitchfork, yet flashed through her mind nonetheless. Her heart began moving with alarming, unnatural urgency.

Hands? This was happening to her because of his *hands?* Then again, there was still the matter of the rest of him. His impact wasn't diminishing despite the amount of time he'd already spent in her office.

"What do you want?" She opened her mouth, and the words fell out, blunt and rattled.

"A few minutes of your time." He closed the distance between them and placed the car back on the model driveway. He did it the way he might handle one of the birds he was so hell-bent on saving lately—the ones he'd tried to grab her land for. He had gentle, forceful hands, Danielle thought, and she shivered.

She hadn't shivered in, well, maybe forever. *She was losing her mind.*

"Here's the part where you acknowledge my request," he suggested. "A simple yes or no will suffice."

Danielle cleared her throat. "You can have fifteen minutes."

"I'll use it wisely then." He slid those hands into his trouser pockets. "You know, I thought you'd be more glib. A wizard with words. A great verbal fencer. That's what they say about you."

Danielle recovered a little more. "I am, but you just walked right in." She frowned. "You startled me, and that put me at a disadvantage."

"Ah." He made the word vibrate with pure masculine satisfaction. "I did that, yes."

"It was rude." What, she wondered, was that cologne he was wearing?

"Should I go out and come back in? Start all over again and do it right?"

"Don't be ridiculous." Danielle tried for her trademark glib charm and waved a hand. "Have a seat. My secretary's gone for the day. That means there's no coffee." She wanted to mention that most people met on matters such as this during regular business hours. But to be fair, he'd requested several appointments with her and she'd declined all of them.

Danielle went to an entertainment center of gleaming black wood built into the wall next to the windows. She stooped to the lower level and opened a small snack bar there, half of it given over to a compact refrigerator. "I can offer you bottled water, a soft drink, papaya juice or scotch." She straightened again to face him. She had herself together now.

"Good scotch?" he asked.

"Absolutely."

"And you're having?"

She heard Richard's voice whispering in her mind, imparting implacable lessons as he always had. He had been gone for three years now but he could still pop into her head at times like this. *Never drink while you're doing business, my dear. Just pretend you are, in order to be sociable. You don't want your head to get muddled.* She wouldn't mind Max Padgett's mind going a little soft for the next fifteen minutes or so, Danielle decided.

She didn't intend for him to stay any longer than that. "Scotch," she said.

Max Padgett nodded. "I'll join you."

She took two crystal glasses from an overhead shelf and began to make the drinks. Max watched her, contemplating this turn of events.

He'd expected her to show him the door, maybe call security to make sure he went on his way, not offer him a drink. Grace under fire, he thought, appreciating it. She wasn't much like he'd anticipated at all.

He'd seen her picture in the papers a few times. None of them had done her justice. Her hair was inky black and reasonably short, curling gently at her collar. She wore it tucked behind seashell ears that wore large diamond studs. She was surprisingly petite—all the photographs he had seen of her had given the impression of more stature. She couldn't be more than five foot two. She was slender as a reed and moved like one giving way to the wind. She wore gold-rimmed eyeglasses that kept trying to slide down her nose as she looked into the scotch tumblers. Cute.

She put a bare splash of scotch in her own glass, more than an inch and a half in his, and topped both off with water at the wet bar. Max grinned to himself. Petite or not, she wanted an edge here, and she was enough the corporate warrior to do what she had to do to get it.

When she made a move toward her desk, he settled into the deep leather chair in front of it. He accepted the glass she passed to him and watched her relax into her own chair. She leaned back coolly, one very elegant leg coming up to cross over the other. She held her own glass in her lap with both hands, and her long, manicured fingers wrapped around it with a smooth ease that gave him a moment's pause and kicked at his pulse.

Damned if the lady didn't have an effect on him. It would make their war interesting, he thought.

"Where were we?" she asked.

"Hmm, we were about to discuss birds."

She nodded sagely. "Let me start for you."

"By all means." So civilized, he thought.

"You're here to fight for your little plovers."

She was too polished to sneer, he realized, but on any other woman, that was what her expression would be called. "Semipalmated," he added.

"Palm what?" Danielle jolted. She looked back at his hands again, watching one lift his drink to his mouth, suddenly mesmerized, just as she'd begun to get her footing. She drank from her own glass quickly and deeply.

"My little plovers are the semipalmated variety," Max explained.

"Of course."

"They're currently reduced to a population of less than five thousand. But you knew that."

"You've pointed it out to me in your many, many letters."

"Enterprises such as yours are killing them off."

"I'm sorry." *What was she saying?* He was getting to her. She knew better than to show any edge of weakness. Danielle rallied. "I have one little enterprise. There are obscene gobs of them up and down the California coast. Why don't you go pick on someone else?"

"Because those resorts are already in existence. That damage is done. *You* I can stop. You haven't broken ground yet."

Her chin came up like a challenge. "We'll do it on May first."

"Not if I can help it."

"That's my point. You can't. I've met all zoning ordinances and every other requirement. There's no sense in bickering about this any longer. I won."

"Oh, I agree. The bickering stage is over. Now it's time for some hand-to-hand combat."

Hand-to-hand? Danielle felt the room spin away.

She looked into his eyes, a cool, gentle blue beneath dark hair. They seemed amused now. For a single, gripping moment she wondered if he somehow knew how he was affecting her, what she was thinking.

Her office was unbearably warm. Her secretary must have nudged the thermostat up again. Danielle got to her feet to check. The thermostat was set at sixty-eight.

"I'd appeal to your good will," he continued, speaking to her over his shoulder, "but you don't have any."

"Of course I do."

"No one has mentioned it." He leaned forward to place his drink on her desk. "Let me tell you what *I* know about you, then we can get back to my plovers."

"Palm plovers."

"Semipalmated." He grinned again and got to his feet to pace her office. Danielle went quickly to sit.

"You're shrewd, calculating and you always land on your feet," he began. "You married Richard Harrington when you were twenty-six, straight out of Stanford with your M.B.A. He was twenty years your elder. Your mother passed away when you were twelve. Your father—Michael Dempsey—was a labor union leader of some renown. You made the rounds with him. You were his shadow all through your youth. You learned the ropes early on."

"Thank you."

Max raised a brow at that, not sure if she was appreciative of his comments regarding her father or herself.

Something happened briefly to her eyes. He thought a shadow moved there. "Richard—your husband—taught you everything he knew," he continued, watching her closely.

"I only wish."

"He died three years ago and you inherited from him obscene business assets."

"His daughter got a portion."

"But you bought her out."

She engaged his eyes, then took another quick sip of scotch. "True."

"Now you're the uncontroverted CEO of Harrington Resorts and Enterprises, Ltd., something you've been groomed for all your life."

"That's about the size of it," Danielle agreed. She didn't tell him that she'd absorbed her father's teachings almost by osmosis. She'd been by his side mostly for photo opportunities.

"They say all you care about is the bottom line," Maxwell said.

That stung a little. "Close, but not quite."

"And you're alone now."

She jumped in her chair as though he had touched her, but when she looked at him, he was studying the model of the resort. Her heart kicked. Had he *said* that—or had she imagined it? Again she had the panicky feeling that he could somehow see inside her head. *Alone* had been a cold place inside her through too many years of her life to count.

That had definitely gotten a reaction out of her, Max thought, watching her through his peripheral vision. "The Gold Beach resort is the first you've done entirely by yourself."

"Insofar as from start to finish, that's correct." But she spoke with less than her usual force, he noticed.

"What a shame. It would have been spectacular."

"It's going to be a doozy."

He laughed aloud. "What do your friends call you?"

"Why?" she asked, startled.

"Danielle? Sir? M'lady?"

"Danielle."

"Ah."

This time that single word slid over her skin like warm velvet. "Ah, what?" she asked suspiciously.

"Just, ah. May I call you Dani? I think it suits you more." Danielle was the woman he'd just described, he thought. Dani would volley about words like *doozy*.

"No!"

Maxwell laughed again. "Then, m'lady, I will tell you this. Assuming your new resort was actually to come into being, you'd want the entrance to face the sea."

"I would?" Danielle sat up straighter in her chair, eyeing him.

"Imagine the view during a good storm that keeps people inside."

He had a point and she liked it.

"Unfortunately," he continued, "this resort cannot possibly come into being because if it does, it will destroy untold unborn semipalmated plovers. The birds are indigenous to Alaska and western Canada, but they migrate twice yearly to South America and back again. And Gold Beach is one of their very favorite places to stop and nest along the way. Particularly, *your* section of Gold Beach."

"They'll be welcome, of course." Danielle sat back in her chair again. "Our low-end rooms will start at $175 a night."

He brought the bottle of scotch back to her desk and topped hers off without adding water. Danielle nudged it away carefully, her hands a little unsteady as he leaned across her desk toward her.

"I think that's out of their price range," he murmured.

She forced a shrug. He was too close. "I'm sorry. I can't help them then."

"Where else will they go?"

"Jonas Patterson's place in Monterey?"

He grinned, but this time it was a fast look, gone almost before it started. It showed teeth. "The birds only visit in the spring and fall. They should return to that beach any day now. When you break ground on May first, you're going to destroy every egg they put down. Don't kill them off, Dani. Have a heart."

She shot to her feet. Maybe it was because he had called her Dani. Maybe it was the fact that he'd remained close enough to her to breathe her air. Or maybe it was only because his suggestion was outrageous. "You honestly expect me to scrap a thirty-million-dollar project because of some *birds?*"

"Honestly," he agreed.

"You're crazy!"

"As a loon."

"How did that species get into this?"

"Actually, I saved them, too, at a lake atop Junipero Sierra Peak five years ago."

"You're a regular Birdman of California, aren't you?"

"I'm an environmental lobbyist."

"And environmental issues are Stanley J. Roberson's platform. What a coincidence."

"Not really."

That surprised her. He was honest. She liked it.

"Maybe you should tell him to stick to the state budget."

"I can't save that for him and I never promised I would." Maxwell finally left her desk and strode across the room, back to the model.

Danielle looked down into her glass. Somehow it had gotten into her hand again and now it was empty. She had probably consumed more scotch in the last half hour than she had in the previous three years combined.

And Max Padgett was looking better by the mouthful.

"This is absurd," she muttered, not sure if she was speaking of the birds or the way his grin softened his mouth, the way he had her *reacting*.

"You won't end up thinking so."

She looked up again quickly. "Is that a threat?"

"More or less."

"With what? I'm legal! That sight is clean, totally permitted, ready to go!"

"But it won't go because deep in your heart you know I'm right about this." He paused and looked at her steadily. "Take a step back, Dani. Think it over. If you proceed, you'll have a substantial fight on your hands. This was a courtesy call. After this, things get ugly."

"You can't seriously think I'll accommodate you on this. It makes absolutely no fiscal sense, and I have board members to report to!"

"It was worth a try."

"So was looking for life on Mars but no one seriously thought they'd find it there."

"Call me a dreamer."

And wouldn't *that* go with those blue eyes. Danielle shook her head as something soft tried to fill it. "My answer is no."

"So it's on to round two then. But Dani." He trailed

off and moved to the door, opened it and looked back at her. "Don't take anything that happens from here on in personally. Just for the record, it turns out that I like you."

"That's m'lady to you." Her intelligent, calculating, CEO knees nearly buckled.

He chuckled, a sound that was rich and warm and golden, then he stepped through the door again and was gone.

Danielle's stomach jittered. It felt as if it had suddenly filled with a hundred fluttering...well, plovers. She'd read somewhere—probably in all that literature he'd sent her—that they darted after their food when they were hungry. Her *nerves* were darting. She sank back down into her chair again, dazed.

What had just happened here? Pure, sizzling, instant chemical attraction, she answered herself. It scared her to death. She didn't know quite what to do with it.

But she liked it.

Chapter Two

"He wants you to call off the resort because of those *birds?*"

Danielle's secretary stood openmouthed in the center of her office early the next morning. Angelique was a stunning, statuesque and shrewd blonde who proved that looks didn't necessarily preclude brains or vice versa. When Richard had first hired her, Danielle had felt the requisite kick of wifely alarm. Then she had gotten to know her.

Three years ago, when Richard had passed on, Danielle had moved her own lackluster secretary into the PR department and had kept Angelique on to work for her. Over time, they'd become friends, eschewing all Richard's whispered warnings in Danielle's head that it wasn't wise to become overly intimate with the staff. The business was all Danielle had. There was no one outside it for her to confide in, worry with, to clap for her victories. Without Angelique, Danielle knew she would be isolated in her ivory tower.

Maxwell Padgett's words shot back to her. *And you're alone now.* She shook them off.

"Actually, I think it's all political." Danielle sipped papaya juice. Twelve hours after the scotch, she still had a headache. Twelve hours after Maxwell Padgett had made his departure, her insides still hummed.

Angelique thought about that and nodded. "Senator Roberson promised something during his campaign about preserving that area of coastline."

"Yes." And the public knew that with Maxwell Padgett and his coalition in his corner, Roberson could deliver on such promises. It had gotten Roberson elected by a narrow margin. What he'd had over his opponent was his close relationship with the powerful lobbyist who could be trusted to push through the legislation Roberson wrote.

Still, Danielle had stood tough against both of them for months. But now she had actually met Maxwell Padgett and that put a different spin on things. Her blood shivered again.

"How do you do it?" she asked suddenly. "How do you draw men like bees to honey?" It was one of Angelique's gifts. Longevity in relationships was not.

Angelique poured herself a mug of coffee and frowned at her. "Why do you want to know?"

Just for the record, it turns out that I like you. Remembering Max's words, she recalled the skitter of excitement that had gone through her. She wanted to feel more of that, Danielle thought, whatever had been going through her blood since twenty past six last night. "I've decided I want one."

Angelique went still. "But you were married to Richard." Angelique rarely made such inane observations which, Danielle supposed, only showed how much she'd surprised her. And what did *that* say for the state of her life?

"Of course I was," Danielle said. "Three years ago. You're the one who keeps telling me that you think I need to get out more."

"I know. I did. I do." Angelique drank from her mug. "I guess I meant...with friends. I seem to have this image of you and Richard still welded together, in the back of my brain."

"He's gone now," Danielle said quietly. And, she thought, she had never felt like this with Richard. Not once, not for a second or a minute or an hour. She'd met him during her last year in graduate school when he'd lectured to one of her classes. He'd invited her for a cup of coffee afterward, and they'd eased into a comfortable, steady courtship that had turned into a comfortable, steady marriage. It had lasted for seven quiet years until he had died. He'd taught her, praised her, admired her...and yes, in many ways he'd welded her to his side where nothing or no one could do her harm or touch her too closely.

This was different.

This was...*lust,* Danielle thought. It was chemistry, with a zing here and a wallop there. It was fireworks on the Fourth of July going off in her brain. It was possibility—open, endless possibility—a feeling of being utterly alive. Maxwell's *hands!* And that grin. His eyes! Her heart rolled over.

She'd been in awe of Richard from the first moment she'd met him, but he had never once made her forget herself and drink two scotch and waters. Their marriage had been a placid pond compared to a churning ocean. Max Padgett was tidal waves, and she had only just realized that she didn't know how to swim.

"Okay, I can deal with this," Angelique mused. "You are, after all, still a young woman."

Danielle glanced at her. "Well, thank you for that." She was only thirty-six.

"Are we talking about any specific man here?"

"Maxwell Padgett."

Angelique's jaw dropped all over again. "This is about the bird man?"

"Who did you think I was talking about? Will you help me?"

"To do what exactly?"

"I don't know…to acquire his interest."

Angelique was instantly alarmed. "Acquire? A man isn't some property you can buy! If you want him, you have to lure him."

"Lure?" Danielle paused, frowning. "Okay. But I need a plan."

"A plan is exactly what you *don't* need."

"I want to set my goals and figure out how best to effectuate them."

"No! With men, you just have to sort of…you know, feel your way along. A plan would scare the death out of 90 percent of them. If Max even smells a plan—" Angelique broke off and snapped her fingers. "Gone."

"No plan?" Danielle repeated faintly. She was definitely out of her depth here.

"No, just a few minor adjustments to start with. The first thing you need to do is plunk down a million or so into some kind of sanctuary for those little feathered friends of his."

"A *million?*" She was shocked. "That's ridiculous! They're plovers!"

"It will look sincere. And he feels strongly about them. Besides, Richard left you with more money than

you could spend in a lifetime even if you weren't raking
in your own huge salary.''

That was true. Danielle hesitated, then she nodded. It
seemed like a lot, but Angelique knew about such things.
She was never without a man.

"It will make him happy," Angelique continued,
"and it will buy us some time to get rid of these suits
you always wear.''

"Richard loved my suits!''

"What do you want here, Danielle? Another solid
marriage or scintillating passion?''

"Passion," she said quickly. But she thought *both*.
Then again, she'd already been blessed with the first,
had never enjoyed the second, so maybe this wasn't the
time to split hairs.

"Go shopping this weekend," Angelique advised. "If
you want to catch his attention, you'll need to drop the
professional ice a little. Until then, stall him. That's my
best advice for now.'' Angelique went to the office door
in a swirl of blond curls. Danielle studied her electric-
blue skirt and the clever white sweater that stopped just
at her waist. "By the way, what are you going to do
about the groundbreaking?''

"I'm going ahead with it," Danielle said quickly.

"Good.''

"If I back down too soon he won't have any excuse
to try to talk me into changing my mind.''

Angelique rolled her eyes and went outside to her
desk in the little anteroom just outside the office. Danielle sat at her own desk. She picked up a pen, then put
it down again. She hugged herself and sighed.

"Danielle Harrington has established some kind of
plover fund to the tune of a half million dollars," Roger

Kimmelman said. "She says you can use it to buy them different land."

Max looked up at his aide then he sat back, laced his fingers behind his head and put his feet up on his desk. "They don't want different land. They want Gold Beach."

Roger nodded. He was all squeaky-clean professionalism, with blond hair perfectly coiffed. His white shirt and dark trousers were pressed razor-sharp. Roger wanted Max's job.

That was fine with Max. At thirty-nine, he fully acknowledged that he wasn't sure exactly what he wanted to do with the rest of his life. He cared about the environment, about the earth that his generation would leave to the next. He thought he could do some good for California during Stan Roberson's term. But politics was not particularly what he wanted to do for a lifetime.

He finally shrugged and dropped his hands. "We can't blame her for trying."

"She's weaseling," Roger said firmly.

"Maybe, maybe not."

"She hasn't announced a delay in her groundbreaking ceremonies."

"She wouldn't. Not yet." Somehow, though he barely knew her, he was sure of that. It would be too easy and not her style. Then Max smiled.

It was Friday. Three days had passed since his unannounced visit to her. It was time to step things up a notch. "Start making those phone calls and we'll implement Plan B. Let's see what we can do by five o'clock."

"That's excellent, sir! We'll get in the last coup with the press before the weekend."

Max honestly didn't care too much about coups. He

cared about the plovers. And, he realized, he was looking forward to seeing Dani Harrington again.

She was a captivating woman. She had a quick wit, an amusing charm. *This* would certainly bring her down to Gold Beach in a hurry, he thought. Max rose from his desk, still grinning.

Danielle was on the telephone with the head of her advertising department when Angelique burst into the room, then slammed the door behind her hard.

"What is it?" Danielle asked, alarmed.

"There are 432 people out there protesting!"

Danielle hung up quickly and came to her feet. "Out where?"

"At the site! At Gold Beach. They're protesting for the plovers. They're carrying *placards!*"

"But I gave him half a million dollars until I could go shopping!"

"Five hundred thousand?" Angelique pressed her hands to the sides of her head. "I told you to humor him! I told you a million! Now all you've done is wave a red flag in front of a bull!"

"Well, it's too late now." Danielle spun away from her desk. *What had gone wrong here?*

"Channel 3 is covering it," Angelique reported, "but I'm sure the other networks will be jumping in shortly."

"Channel 3 interrupted regular programming for *this?* They're just birds!" Danielle was shocked. She rushed to the entertainment center. Obviously, Maxwell was accelerating the game, she thought. But she wasn't prepared!

Just for the record, it turns out that I like you. Was it possible that *he* just wanted to see *her* again? There were simpler ways to go about it!

Danielle punched on the television. She switched to Channel 3, and his wonderful, enticing face filled the screen. It was windy out at the site today. One lock of dark hair fell forward over his brow. The gusts lifted it, kicked it, put it back again. She wanted to touch it.

"What are you going to do?" Angelique fretted.

Danielle brought herself back and looked at her secretary. "I have to put in an appearance before the rest of the television stations get there, but let's see what he has to say first." She reached and turned up the volume.

"Ms. Harrington must be made to understand that money does not buy lives!" Max Padgett announced— passionately, she thought. "The earth is our precious commodity! When the plovers return to this site, what will they possibly spend Harrington money on? All they'll want is their nests, their chicks!"

"Ouch," Danielle muttered. Then she narrowed her eyes and glared at the television screen. He was turning things all around! That money would buy his birds plenty of land to lay their nests on!

"Scrap the project! Scrap the project!" chanted the placard-carrying crowd behind him.

Still, there was a moral element at play here, Danielle realized. She pressed her hand to her heart. She wished desperately for some of Richard's advice right now, but the memory of his voice was silent.

"Okay," she muttered. "I can fix this. Call the other networks. Tell them that if they wait half an hour they'll get some real footage, because I'll be there to confront him. I can't let him have all those cameras to himself."

"Right." Angelique yanked the door open again.

"And get Research and Development to do some fast—*very* fast—digging. I need to know everything there is to know about that stretch of beach by the time

I get out there. I need some ammunition now that he's taking this public.''

Her secretary went out. Danielle headed after her, then she froze in midstride. She was—of course—wearing a suit.

This wouldn't do.

She could save the site. She was good at that. But she wasn't dressed—according to Angelique's advice—for getting her man, to boot. She left her office and stopped at Angelique's desk.

"I need clothes."

Angelique replaced the telephone she had just picked up. "There's no time." She paused. "You just need cleavage."

Danielle ripped away the patterned silk scarf she had tucked in at her throat.

"Okay, good. If we can get rid of the slacks, we might have something."

"I have some clothes here!"

"Is there a skirt? Change the pants for a skirt, then you'll just have to go for it."

Danielle hurried back to her office, to the closet tucked into a discreet corner. She pawed through the clothing there. Black, she decided. Her suit jacket was crimson. At least it would make a dramatic contrast. She yanked a skirt off its hanger, then she peeled out of her slacks. She dragged the skirt back up again. She had ankle-high boots on, she realized, and the skirt was as short as an octogenarian's memory. Now she remembered why she had left it here. She'd considered it inappropriate and had gone out to buy a more suitable one just before a board meeting a few months ago. She'd never taken this one home again because it just wasn't her style.

But that had been before Maxwell Padgett had crusaded his way into her life.

Danielle left her office again and ran to the elevator. "No, wait!" she heard Angelique cry behind her. "Those boots!"

"I'll take care of it."

She jogged down the hallway. At the elevator, the head of her R&D department caught her. "Keep your cell phone on. I think we might have some interesting information on the senator."

Danielle nodded jerkily and stepped into the elevator rushing out when it landed at the subterranean garage floor. Her keys were already in her hand. She fumbled blindly for the remote to raise the top of her convertible because there would be no place at Gold Beach for her to comb her hair before she faced the television cameras.

Before she reached the vehicle, the ragtop rose overhead and settled nicely into place. She didn't bother to slap the locks shut. She dove into the driver's seat and unzipped the ankle-high boots, using her toes to pry them off her feet. Then she jammed the key into the ignition and hit the gas. As she maneuvered her way down the coastal highway, she tossed the boots over her shoulder into the little well of space behind the seats. What the hell? Cameras never caught anything below the waist anyway.

Now she was ready for him.

Channels 4 and 10 were still down at the street, angling their cameras toward town in big, panoramic shots. She'd probably gotten through to the networks and told them she was going to make an appearance, Max decided. That was only fair.

Behind him, his protestors continued to chant and

march. And here came an emerald-green BMW Roadster. Maxwell knew before it reached the site and stopped that it would be her. The car suited her—it was different, rich and smart looking. An image filled his head of the top down, that black hair of hers dancing in the wind. Her clear blue eyes would come alive. In his imagination, Max switched her gold-rimmed spectacles for sporty sunglasses. He wondered if she liked the speed of the car or just its lines and the open air.

Then the car's brakes gave an indignant squeal and its convertible top blew up jerkily. She emerged from the vehicle like a female Poseidon rising from the sea...angry, magnificent, glorious.

Something punched solidly into Max's gut, taking his air. He loved women—the tastes of them, their scents, their quicksilver moods. He most especially loved to enjoy them, then go home alone to run the good parts through his mind a second time. Then he let go. He kept things light and friendly. He never let himself get too attracted to any of them. It was something he had long accepted and understood about himself. At least, he thought he had...until Danielle Harrington came out of her car.

She wore crimson and black. The neckline of her jacket plunged deeply. As she drew closer, he saw something peeking out at the V. It was fire-engine red, a shade deeper than the jacket.

Lace? *She wore fire-engine red underwear.*

His eyes roved down. Her skirt was short and narrow. And below that, she was barefoot. This was a new side of the woman he'd read about and had finally met three days ago. Max dropped his own placard at his feet as she reached his side and glared up at him.

"This was sneaky and underhanded!" she charged.

He tried to gather his thoughts. "That's not true. I warned you up-front that things were about to get ugly."

"You could have bought those birds gold-plated nests with all the money I donated!"

"The plovers don't want gold. They want the same land they've been squatting on for generations."

"Ha! There! You see? That is precisely my point. They're *squatting*. This is my land. I bought it fair and square."

"Bottom line again, Dani?"

It hurt. She sucked in her breath. "Go to hell. And don't call me Dani."

She was definitely riled, he thought. Temper crackled about her like electricity. She snatched her glasses from her eyes and turned to wave a hand at the news cameras down at the street. The mob rolled toward them.

"My resort will provide jobs, revenue, tax dollars to this county," she said when they reached them. "Mr. Padgett is being fanatical. He certainly doesn't have the *people's* best interest at heart if he attempts to stall this project!"

All eyes—and all the cameras—swivelled to him. Max pulled his gaze from the red bra showing at the swell of her breasts. What had happened here? Suddenly she was absolute, outrageous, mouth-watering sex.

On television?

It didn't matter where they were or who was watching. He had never wanted anything more in his life than to topple her here, now, into the sand and steep himself in her. And with her cheeks flushed like that, she looked as if he'd just done exactly that. He very nearly had a visible reaction to that little fantasy right on network news.

"Mr. Padgett?" someone called out.

"What?" He looked quickly back at the cameras.

"Can you give us a reaction to Ms. Harrington's suggestion?"

Ms. Harrington had made a suggestion?

She turned to face him and cocked one hip. Max leaned closer to her. "You're practically naked," he said in an undertone.

"I am not!" But her hand fluttered up as though tug at her neckline before she dropped it again quickly. "You're just trying to distract me."

"It's called leveling the playing field." It was also called stalling. *What the hell had she said to the press?*

"I don't want it level. I want to win."

"You told me on Tuesday that you already had."

"That was before I realized you wouldn't concede graciously."

"I never led you to believe I would."

They were nearly nose to nose. The scent she wore made him think of ocean mist, gentle and clinging. It filled his head. Her eyes snapped with blue fire now. For the longest while not one member of the media said a word. Max realized suddenly that the cameras were soaking this up, and he took a quick, precise step back to put distance between them again.

And even so, he could still see a peek of that lace.

He waited for her to say something else. He needed some kind of clue as to what had transpired while he'd been fantasizing about making love to her in the sand. But she only crossed her arms beneath her breasts. The pressure puffed the edges of her lapels out a bit, giving him a good view of some very nice swells and contours. His blood started hammering all over again.

"I dare you to deny it," she challenged.

He would...if he had any clue at all what it was that he was supposed to be denying.

Danielle swung back to the cameras. Her arms dropped to her sides again and that was a shame. Then she threw a look back at him over her shoulder. Her mouth curved in a clever little smile. And was that an *invitation* in her eyes?

"The ball's in your court, Mr. Padgett," she murmured.

What ball? What court? Where? She turned and began picking her way across the dunes again, toward her car. If there was anything more provocative than the way a woman moved when walking barefoot in sand, Max thought, then he didn't know what it was. He missed three or four more questions shot at him by the media as he watched her.

"Is it true?" someone from Channel 4 asked.

Max looked back at the cameramen and reporters, feeling dazed. "I'm certainly going to, uh, look into it."

Satisfied, ready to move on to other, beefier news, the media began to pack up and depart. Even as Danielle's emerald-green Roadster revved and sped off, Max saw Roger Kimmelman's sedate gray Chrysler pull into the spot she had vacated. Max jogged over to meet his aide halfway when Roger got out of the car.

"What did she say?" Max demanded.

"Who?" Roger looked at him oddly.

"Danielle Harrington. Here. Just now. To the cameras."

"You were standing right next to her."

"I was distracted."

"By what?"

Max opened his mouth and closed it again firmly.

Roger's frown deepened. "She says your birds can

nest on the senator's land. You could even use her donated half million to buy it.''

Max felt his heart fall hard and fast. It landed in his gut with a thud. "What land?"

"That land over there."

Roger pointed. Max's gaze moved reluctantly in that direction.

"You're telling me that that stretch of beach belongs to *Stan?*" he asked.

"It's not something that would have come to the coalition's attention unless the owner decided to build on it," Roger said indignantly, as though Max had somehow implied that this nightmare was his fault. "We can't be expected to police the ownership of every scrap of beach, every field and stream in California, just in case someone *might* decide to do something with it. There are too many battles to fight without inviting ones that aren't even an issue yet!"

It was true, Max thought. His lobby rushed in when nature was in danger of being spoiled, raped and ruined by the cancerous spread of civilization. Along this coastline, only Harrington Resorts was threatening that.

Then he had another thought. His heart chugged in alarm. "Did she tell the cameras that Stan was going to build here?"

"She certainly implied it."

Of course she would, Max thought. This part of the beach was outside the city limits, and anyone planning to develop it needed the power companies to extend their services out this far. The companies would demand an astronomical price for the favor. That was what had protected the land from development for so long. But now Dani Harrington had footed the worst of the bills, and it

was logical to infer that other owners would jump in and
start building also.

Max rubbed at a headache growing behind his forehead. It was time to have a talk with the man who was
the closest thing to a brother he would ever know. But
Max looked the way Danielle's car had gone instead.

Damned if he hadn't just been sucker punched by a
woman in red underwear.

Chapter Three

Was that *her?* She looked like a...a *harlot!*

Danielle stood rooted in the middle of her bedroom, clutching the VCR remote in both hands. She shuddered in her thin silk robe, more from shock than the fact that, with usual April capriciousness, the weather had taken a turn back into winter by the time she'd gotten home from the site.

Angelique had dropped off a video tape she'd made of the broadcast. Now, right there on television, Danielle watched her own neckline plunge and her lapels gape. Then the camera pulled back for a wide-angle shot and the public saw more of her legs than her husband probably had in the seven years they'd been married.

What had she done?

When the telephone rang, Danielle jumped and pivoted to the night table. She reached for it, then her hand went still. *What if it was a board member?* She pressed her fingers to her temples as the phone kept shrilling.

She had a responsibility to so many people and she

had always projected a cool, capable image to all of them. Now she'd been caught on all three networks parading around in her underwear.

Danielle took in a deep breath and finally picked up the phone. "Hello?"

"Did you watch it yet?" Angelique demanded.

Danielle let her air out. "Half of it."

"You were perfect."

"I was—" She broke off, stunned. "What?"

"Watch his eyes!"

Danielle spun back to the television and aimed the remote to freeze the screen. Her own image was nose-to-nose with Maxwell's in the frame. She remembered this part. It was when she had accused him of not conceding. She'd thought—then—that he'd been staring her right in the eyes—and his hadn't been cool and clever and amused in that moment. They had been so intent she'd felt the impact of them like a physical touch. But she'd thought it was his temper that had changed them. Now—here, in this frame—she realized that he wasn't looking into her eyes at all.

He was looking…downward. At her breasts. And the smoke in his gaze had nothing whatsoever to do with plovers.

A steady quaking started inside her. It had worked. Angelique's advice had worked!

"You'll be hearing from him soon," Angelique promised. "I give it forty-eight hours at the outside. Just look at him. He can't even breathe."

She couldn't breathe. Danielle pounded a fist against her chest to jumpstart her heart.

In that moment, if only for that moment, Max Padgett had definitely been interested in what he was seeing. Excitement leaped in her, hot and expectant, then it shredded apart. There was still the matter of her board members. And the plovers. She had a mess on her hands, and for the first time in her entire thirty-six years, her hormones were in overdrive. She could barely even think coherently. Danielle hung up numbly, then the line rang again.

Her heart vaulted. Was it him? Already? No, of course not. He didn't have her home phone number. She picked up anyway. "Yes?"

"A truly inspired approach!" came the robust voice of Albert Tresca, one of the board members. "You never gave him a chance to build up any steam at all! Is it true? Does Senator Roberson own that land?"

"So says our R & D department." Would he mention the way she had looked?

"I wonder if Richard ever really knew what he had in you."

She winced. Did he mean professionally or—she cringed away from the thought—personally?

"What's next?" Tresca asked. "What else have you got up your sleeve?"

Danielle reached for her usual businesslike tone. Then the words she'd been about to say got jammed in her throat.

An idea leaped into her mind. Her gaze flew back to the television, to the video shot that remained frozen there. Max Padgett was still looking downward. His gaze was still smoky. Danielle's heart slammed against her chest.

This attraction between them could be useful.

What if she used that angle? Could she keep that awareness going and keep his mind off the plovers? Was it possible?

"Are you still there?" Tresca asked.

"I'm here," she answered a little hoarsely. "I...I have a thought but I'm not ready to share it yet." She said goodbye quickly and dropped the phone back into its cradle. Then she picked it up again to leave it off the hook.

Was she actually thinking of *seducing* him? No, she decided quickly, of course not. But she could certainly sidetrack him a little with...well, with feminine wiles. Why not? He certainly hadn't been his usual forceful and confident self in front of those cameras this afternoon. Except...

Except it was outrageous. It was the kind of thing that gave women entrepreneurs a bad name. And it definitely wasn't her usual method. What would Richard think? That—and the fact that she had no *other* brilliant ideas about how to proceed with the plover problem from here—finally sobered her.

Danielle went unsteadily to the central staircase of the echoing old home she had shared with Richard. She thought for the thousandth time that she really ought to sell the place and find a smaller home. She'd simply been too busy with Harrington Resorts these past three years to do anything about it. All her life she'd craved a tidy home with a neat lawn and window boxes full of flowers instead of these lavish and ornate gardens. In her heart she saw something white with green shutters, maybe with an elm and a few bicycles in the yard. Richard had never made any bones about the fact that he'd already raised his family. They had never planned to have children. They'd had the business together; *that* was their baby.

It had only made sense, but sometimes lately it left her feeling hollow. If there had been a child, she wouldn't be so alone now. If there had been one, these halls wouldn't echo with silence but with laughter.

Danielle found her way into the parlor. She inhaled deeply, and for the first time realized that the lingering aroma of Richard's pipe had finally faded, just as the scent of her father's cologne had finally left his favorite shirt after he'd died, just as she'd finally stopped smelling her mother's Irish stew in the kitchen long after Carolyn Dempsey had departed this earth. She curled up in Richard's favorite chair and propped her chin in her hand.

She wondered exactly how one went about wooing a man once his attention was caught.

The cue ball cracked into the eight ball with a sound that split the quiet of the room. Max watched the billiard drop into a pocket. "My game," he said.

"It was close, though," Stan Roberson replied. They'd grown up together on some of the worst streets of Sacramento and had amused themselves in more pool halls than either of them could count. They were evenly matched.

Max had wanted to annihilate him tonight just on general principle. He was angry.

"You should have told me," he said again, his gaze moving to the television perched in a corner of Stan's rec room ceiling. Stan's staff had—of course—taped the news. Now they were playing the video. Max watched Dani Harrington approach the cameras, all legs, bare feet and hot eyes. It had the same effect on him that it had had earlier in the evening. It felt like something solid, hard and hot hit him in the solar plexus.

Who *was* this woman that she could go from tycoon to siren in the space of three days? What was it about her that she could wipe his mind blank of the business—the *important* business—at hand?

This changed everything.

Stan snapped his fingers in front of Max's gaze. "Come back to me."

"I'm here."

"No, you're not. You're getting all worked up over the woman who's going to make me look like a fool."

Max's temper spiked all over again. "Some might say the fool is the one who sicced me on Gold Beach without telling me he was an owner out there."

"It's not germane to the issue. I don't intend to uproot the plovers, at least not until long after my term is over."

Max's eyes narrowed dangerously. "That's good. Spoken like a true politician."

"I am what I am. And I'll be damned if I'm going back to poor obscurity. I'm telling you, my land isn't an issue here."

"She's making it an issue."

"She won't be able to. *I* haven't applied for any permits to bulldoze plover eggs. I promised to preserve that coastline, and I haven't done anything to fly in the face of that. Ownership isn't a crime, especially if I leave the land wide open for the birds." Stan shook his head. "I'm going to retire out there, Max. I just turned forty. Retirement is a long way off. Besides, Danielle Harrington only found out that I own *one* of those plots. She doesn't seem to realize that I bought two."

"You did *what?*" This was getting worse by the minute, Max thought. Gold Beach was an elliptical area maybe a mile long. He thought the whole of it might be comprised of all of four parcels. "You've got to unload all of it!"

"Let's not be hasty," Stan said. "I'm thinking that

maybe I could cough up one—the one she unearthed the paperwork on—and keep the other.''

Max barely heard him. He was watching the television again. On the screen Danielle drew in a breath to snap something back at him, and he glimpsed that red lace. He rubbed his eyes, pulling his gaze from the TV.

Stan began to rack the balls again. ''Meanwhile, we'll probably need an injunction now. We'll have to stop her in her tracks so we have time to reconnoiter from this. I'll have my staff get on it first thing Monday morning.''

Max picked up his pool stick, then her voice drifted from the television, low and sultry. *''The ball's in your court, Mr. Padgett.''* He looked at the TV and there it was again, that *look* in her eyes.

It was come-hither if he'd ever seen one.

He felt things tighten inside him in response. She was spectacular. She did things to him. He wanted to see more—a lot more—of that red lace. And that scared the hell out of him. It scared him enough that—as much as she'd intrigued him—he sure as hell didn't plan to cross paths with her again. A woman like this was lethal.

He'd spent fifteen of his first seventeen years being shuffled from foster home to foster home. Most people could reflect their opinions of relationships back on one or two sets of parents. Max could base his opinions on six separate couples who had raised him after his mother had died and his father could not be found. He'd learned that people fall out of love—not just occasionally, but commonly. What he knew of love was that two people entered into it with stars in their eyes and the best of intentions. Then there were differences of opinion, one or the other put on a few pounds over the years, and the gloss wore off and self-interest emerged. Everything went to hell in a handbasket. There was fighting and vicious, nasty hurt. And finally, when it was over, there was emptiness, the unique emptiness of finding oneself alone and unloved.

He'd never wanted any part of it. That was why—doggedly and determinedly—he had never in his life gone out with the same woman more than twice. None of them, however, had quite the impact of Dani Dempsey Harrington.

Stan was watching him with thoughtful eyes, Max realized. "What?" he asked suspiciously.

"I guess there's something else I should tell you," Stan said.

"You own land on Junipero Sierra Peak, too?"

"It wouldn't matter. You've already preserved that area. I'm marrying Marcy."

The pool stick dropped from Max's hand and rolled on Stan's thick carpeting. Max stared at him.

"It's time," Stan continued. "We've been together eight years now. She wants it."

"So you're just going to roll over and play dead?" Max was panicked. His pulse started pistoning. The world as he knew it was crumbling at his feet. A woman had turned up on the beach to make every drop of blood in his veins race and burn with a kind of hunger that had wanted to be assuaged *now*. And his best friend was getting *married*.

Stan grinned. "It will be a sweet death."

"It's a career move, right?"

"It's a life move, Max. I want you to be my best man."

Max opened his mouth and found he couldn't answer. He replaced his stick in the rack.

Stan grinned. "Take it easy. You'll recover from the shock by morning. And as soon as you do, you've got to call Danielle Harrington and start unraveling this mess.''

His stomach somersaulted. "I don't *want* to call Danielle Harrington.''

"We have to meet with her and cool her down.'' Stan cracked the balls whether Max wanted to play or not.

Then the door opened and Marcy Leeds poked her head into the room. "Stan? Are you almost through in here?''

Max watched his best friend grin like a besotted puppy. "In a minute, hon.'' And then *she* gave a come-hither smile before she retreated, Max thought.

He had to get out of here.

"All right,'' Max muttered. "I'll call Dani Harrington tomorrow.'' But he damned well wasn't going to like it.

Danielle was in the middle of a meeting at ten-thirty on Monday morning, recapping the current status of the war between Harrington Resorts and the Coalition for Wildlife, Fields and Streams, when Angelique knocked on the conference room door and stepped into the room. "You told me to interrupt you.''

"I did?'' Danielle remembered nothing of the sort.

"This morning. If *he* called.''

"He—oh!'' Danielle's heart stood still for a moment. She looked quickly at the faces surrounding the table. "Max Padgett is on the phone.''

She pushed past Angelique and hurried down the hall to her own office. By the time she reached it, her knees were liquid. She looked down at the blinking light on the phone. Angelique had *almost* been right, she thought. It had taken him seventy-two hours to call…but then, he couldn't have reached her over the weekend even if he had tried. Her home number was unlisted, a well-guarded secret. Richard had been emphatic about business not following them home. She'd never thought to change that. There was no reason to. There wasn't anyone she particularly cared about being able to reach her during nonbusiness hours.

Until now. She made a mental note to ask Angelique to call the telephone company.

Danielle took one, two, then three deep breaths and finally grabbed the receiver. "Hi," she said. Then she covered her eyes with one hand, fighting a moan. She sounded breathless and hormonal and flirtatious, exactly like a woman who would run around on television in her underwear.

"Hi, yourself," Max said, his voice vaguely rough. And she thought *he* sounded as thought he had just come up for air after a long, slow, heated kiss.

Her knees gave out. Danielle sank into her chair.

"Have you come to your senses yet?" he asked.

"And here I thought you were calling to tell me you're giving up."

"It will never happen."

No, she thought, he wouldn't be a quitter. "We have a problem then. I'm not planning to back off, either."

"What are you saying, Dani? That we're evenly matched?"

Something unseen snatched the air from her lungs. "Maybe."

"Let's talk about it."

"Talk." She couldn't breathe. "When?"

"Tomorrow night? Are you free?"

She hadn't had anything *but* a free evening since Richard had died. "Let me check." She put him back on hold.

She inhaled carefully, deliberately, trying to get oxygen to her brain. Then she stabbed the blinking button on her phone again. "I can manage it. I'll have to move a few things around, but this is important."

"That's progress," he said in that low, intimate voice.

"It is?" Her heart hammered.

"A week ago you wouldn't answer my mail or take my phone calls. Could it be I'm gaining ground?"

Not in the way you think. Danielle closed her eyes as the words tumbled to her lips. She pressed a hand to her mouth to keep them trapped. "I'll let you think so."

He laughed that warm whisky-edged chuckle. It came through the wire and touched her skin. "I'm sorry," she said quickly, shivering again. "Could you hold another moment?"

Danielle slammed her palm down on the hold button again. She dragged a shaky hand across her brow. *What was going on here?* She wasn't any good at this...at this flirting business! *Were* they flirting? She didn't know! She'd barely even dated before she'd met Richard— she'd been too busy getting her M.B.A. And she *hadn't* dated since he'd died. He'd been the sum total of her experience with men. And there had been no perspiring brows or weak knees or irregular heartbeats with Richard. So when it came to Max Padgett, she was lost.

All she had were her instincts.

They were definitely flirting, she decided. She thought again of her resolve to use that to keep his mind off the birds, at least long enough for her to break ground. She picked up the phone again. "Where would you like to meet tomorrow night?"

"How about the Angels game?"

"What angels?"

There was a beat of silence. "The baseball team."

"Oh. Of course." A *baseball* game? "That would be fine."

"Stan Roberson has a sky box at the stadium. I'll leave a ticket for you at the gate. Just come up and meet us there."

Us? Stan Roberson? For the first time since she'd heard his voice again, Danielle's CEO antennae twitched and came back to life. "What are you up to?"

"As you pointed out on Friday, Stan *does* own the land next to yours."

"That's not an answer."

And, Max thought on the other end of the line, she was quick enough to realize it, not shy about calling him on it. Damn it, he didn't *want* to like her.

He found himself wondering what she was wearing and if it involved any lace peeking out. Then, appalled, he realized that he'd actually asked the question aloud.

"What?" She didn't sound shocked. She sounded breathless.

He rephrased quickly. "What does a corporate maven wear to celebrate a televised victory?"

"You're conceding that that was a victory?"

"I'm observing that you seem to have a...uh, varied fashion sense."

She'd always stuck to solid, classic fabrics. Apparently, Angelique's advice had been more on target than either of them realized. She *had* to go shopping. Danielle ran a finger inside the collar of her mauve suit jacket. She felt warm. "I'm flexible," she murmured, "about almost everything except plovers."

"Sounds like a promise."

Her heart leaped. "Or a warning."

One he should heed, Max thought. What the hell was he doing? Hadn't he determined to keep this a matter of purely business, keep the focus on land and plovers? "We'll all discuss it tomorrow night. The bird problem," he added quickly.

Danielle steadied herself again. "Senator Roberson doesn't need my cooperation to sell his land to my fund and set it aside for your birds. I gave my accountant power-of-attorney over that money."

"The minute you move a bulldozer in, the plovers will flee Stan's land, as well. The parcels are side by side. These birds are antisocial."

"What a shame."

"I think so. They also won't know where your land stops and Stan's begins. They won't lay their eggs down on Stan's side of a line they can't see."

"Then draw them one."

He was quiet for a thoughtful beat. "You're a cold-hearted woman, Dani Harrington."

She flinched. She'd gone professional again, she realized. So much of it was habit. So much of this ground was new. "I'm just realistic. And don't call me Dani."

"We can discuss that, too." He paused and his voice dropped a notch. "I'm looking forward to it."

"I...yes. Yes, of course."

He disconnected. Danielle fumbled the phone back into its cradle.

She could do this. She just needed...guidelines. Some sort of framework to work within. Angelique was wrong. She *definitely* needed a plan. She was just too far out of her element otherwise. Without one, this would be a disaster.

Angelique's advice had gotten Max's attention. Now that she had it—sort of—she had to do something with it. Except she didn't even know what sort of something she wanted!

Danielle rose unsteadily from her desk, then she sat again. She wanted to sidetrack him, she reminded herself. She wanted to divert him from the land issue. And if she felt this wonderful fluttery feeling in the process, well then, that was fun, too. She'd win this war and have a delightful time doing it.

But first she had to keep his attention, had to figure out how to keep him on his toes. She needed a plan for that, she thought again.

She left her office, stepping into the hall. Like manna from heaven, she saw the head of her public relations department moving toward her, his head down as he read a piece of paper. Richard had always advised her to remember the personal details of their top-level employees. Michael Axler was forty-six years old, and he lived with a significant other named…named…Denise, she remembered.

"Michael, how are you?" Danielle asked. "How is Denise?"

His head came up. His smile was vacant at first, then warmed. "Hi, Ms. Harrington. Denise is fine. Thanks for asking."

"Did I hear she was in the hospital?"

"Minor surgery a month ago. It was no big deal." He started to move past her.

"You know, I always wondered," Danielle said.

"Wondered about what?" He looked back at her with a confused frown.

"You're so…so good together. You and Denise."

He hesitated. "Uh…thank you."

"I was just curious. What made you want to see her again the first time you met her?"

Michael laughed, at ease again. If he thought the question odd, then he wasn't going to show it. "We had everything in common," he answered.

"Everything in common," Danielle repeated. She'd expected to hear something more along the lines of short skirts and great legs.

"A lot of shared interests," Michael clarified. "Listen, I've got to get back to my office, Ms. Harrington. If that's all...?"

"Oh, of course. I'm sorry for keeping you."

"No problem. I'll tell Denise you were asking about her."

"You do that," Danielle murmured.

Shared interests?

It was exactly what had drawn her and Richard together, she reflected. But somehow she had expected to use something more...more volatile and provocative on Max Padgett. All the same, she could handle a few shared interests, she decided, if she only knew what Maxwell's were.

Danielle smacked a hand against her forehead. He had just invited her to a baseball game, hadn't he? *Sports!*

She turned back to her office to get her purse and passed Angelique's desk again. "I've got to go out for a while," she said quickly.

"Now? You were in the middle of a board meeting."

"Tell them I have pressing business with this coalition matter."

"When will you be back?"

How long would it take to turn herself into a sports fan? Danielle didn't know. "Better not count on me until tomorrow."

"You're going to stay out *all day?* You never stay

away all day. And you've got that conference call this afternoon with our Boston property.''

Danielle didn't answer. She set off purposefully down the hallway, leaving her secretary to stare after her.

Chapter Four

At six o'clock on Tuesday night, Danielle stood in front of the cheval mirror in her bedroom with a checklist clenched in her hand. Her heart alternately skipped beats then hammered.

She wasn't sure which rattled her more...trying to use Max's attraction to sidetrack him from the plover issue, or the idea that he even seemed to be attracted to her in the first place. She forced herself to breathe deeply two, three, then four times. She could do this, she told herself. She certainly had enough motivation.

She'd decided that it was a *good* thing that Senator Roberson would be joining them. This was her best chance to convince him to sell his land to her plover fund, and that would pretty much tidy up this whole mess. She'd considered Maxwell's argument that the birds wouldn't know which land was their refuge and which was hers to develop, but she didn't think that was as much of a problem as he was making it out to be. She had no issue with a few nests on her land. She just wanted a resort there, also. And a few plovers darting about would lend the place a certain charm.

As for Maxwell's position that the plovers were shy and wouldn't appreciate the human company, maybe she could establish a large hedgerow or some such thing between the parcels. That would give them a little privacy. She didn't seriously believe they would leave a place where they had been nesting for generations just because there was a hotel next door.

Richard had often told her that she could talk anyone into anything. So yes, she could pull this off, Danielle assured herself. All she had to do was keep Maxwell from swaying the senator over to his side again once she had accomplished her goal.

"Easy as pie," Danielle said aloud, then she relaxed her fist to look at her list again.

Lists were good. They were an excellent tool of organization. Angelique had said nothing about lists. She'd advised against making a *plan,* but this wasn't the same thing. With that in mind, Danielle had asked no less than five men in the mall yesterday what a woman should wear to a baseball game if she wanted to appeal to the man who had invited her.

"Jeans," she read. Actually, that particular suggestion had been for cutoff denim shorts, but she'd been forced to adapt it to fit the circumstances. An April evening on the northern California coast was not a time for cutoffs.

She looked up at her reflection again and smiled a little bemusedly. She'd found the jeans at the very bottom of one of her drawers. She'd bought them years ago to wear while she tinkered in their gardens, but Richard had proved so uncomfortable with her new hobby that she'd given it up. He'd said that that was what he employed gardeners for. Danielle had kept the jeans all the same, though she'd never worn them again until now.

She went back to her list. "One of those short T-shirts." This suggestion had actually been mentioned twice. The second guy had talked about the kind that dipped off one shoulder, but no one in any of the stores Danielle had visited had quite understood what she was asking for when she'd put all this T-shirt advice together. She'd ended up buying a regular one and taking scissors to it.

Now skin showed above the waistband of her jeans. Just a sliver of it, but still, it was skin. Something inside her squirmed, but since she couldn't do the shoulder thing she decided to go with it. In any event, she didn't own any other T-shirts, and something told her a turtleneck was not what those men had had in mind.

"Baseball cap," she read next. That had seemed like a no-brainer until she'd actually attempted to purchase it. There were so *many* of them. She'd finally settled on one with a lot of colorful lines and letters slashing across the front of it. Now she tugged it down on her forehead a little.

She wasn't going to have time to watch the instructional video she'd bought to learn some fundamental aspects of the game. There was no help for it now. She would just have to wing that part of it.

"Take me out to the ball game," she murmured, then she turned away from the mirror. She pushed her glasses up the bridge of her nose out of habit…then she stopped in midstride as she headed for the bedroom door.

She didn't have glasses anymore. She'd traded them in this morning for contact lenses. Glasses had served her well since she'd been fourteen, but now… Well, now she was trying to hold the attention of a man who could seriously derail a thirty-million-dollar resort project, a man who could make her shiver with just the tone of his voice.

Danielle drew in a few more measured breaths, then she snagged her new baseball jacket off the foot of the bed. She pulled it on as she marched from the bedroom, determined.

Her confidence held up until she turned her car into the stadium parking lot. *The cars!* There were thousands of them, she thought. They were everywhere, clogging any available free space where she might have driven. Danielle planted her foot on the brake and stopped the BMW. A parking lot attendant approached to knock on her window. She lowered the glass, and he leaned down to brace his arms on her door.

"You'll have to keep moving along, doll. We've got a lot of people trying to get in behind you."

Doll? Danielle was flabbergasted. No one had ever called her that before in her life! It was the clothes, she thought. It had to be the clothes. This, she thought, was a whole new world. "I'm attending the Angels game," she explained.

"Well, you're in the right place then. Self-park or valet?"

"Valet." She was relieved that they had such a thing here. Her nerves were too alive with the prospect of the evening ahead to worry about all this snarled traffic.

"Straight ahead about thirty yards then turn right. Someone will take the car from you." He started to straighten, then he paused. "By the way, what is it with you chicks and NASCAR?"

"I beg your pardon?" *Chicks? NASCAR?*

"Your cap." He gestured at it.

"Do you like it?" Danielle asked, suddenly worried. Maybe it was too much.

"Sure," he said. "I follow racing."

Racing? Danielle took the cap of her head and looked at the pretty colorful lines again. What did racing have to do with anything?

Another young man took the BMW from her at the valet area. Danielle got out, stretched the nervous kinks out of her muscles, and handed him a tip. "An associate was going to leave a ticket at a gate for me," she said. "Where might that be?"

"Right there, lady." He jabbed a finger in the direction of her left shoulder, then he leaped into the car and revved the motor. "Please!" she cried. "Be gentle with—" But it was too late. He was gone in a flash of emerald-green and growling engine.

Danielle turned toward the stadium. She saw a window in the area where he had pointed. She went and stood in line.

Twenty long minutes later she had her sky box pass. It was in an envelope across which a strong male hand had written *Dani Harrington.* Not Danielle, and there was no trace of the Dempsey she generally included. She laughed aloud. He was certainly persistent. She liked that. Then something squirmed a little inside her, and it wasn't an entirely uncomfortable feeling. She continued to study the envelope.

Dani Harrington. It looked so casual, she thought, so basebally. It sounded like a woman someone might call *doll.* Suddenly, without warning, a yearning hit her...to be just that kind of woman, clever and coquettish, the kind who wouldn't have to ask questions about how to entice a man. A woman a man might be enticed by, regardless. A woman who didn't leave a television on just for the company of other voices.

She shook the feeling off and fell in line with a throng of people moving into the stadium. Inside, she was awed. She stopped and looked around until someone poked her in the spine to get her to move again. She quickly stepped forward to the rail.

The place was *huge!* She'd never seen so many seats before in her life. She'd thought the opera house in San Francisco was big, but this was staggering.

A man balancing an enormous tray of soft drinks against his stomach moved past her. The tray was held in place by a thick strap around his neck. Suddenly Danielle realized she was parched. "Oh, wait," she said. "I'd like one of those."

The man stopped. "Three bucks."

It seemed like an exorbitant amount, but she dug in her purse. "Damn." She'd given her last available cash to the valet man. Richard had always cautioned her not to carry too much of it. It was unnecessary, he'd said. Anything worth buying could always be placed on a credit card whereby the accountant would take care of it at the end of the month. Obviously, he had never attended an Angels game.

She looked around again and couldn't even begin to picture him here. An odd spurt of anger hit her, that she had missed so much because he had deigned it to be beneath them.

"Ma'am?"

"Oh, I'm sorry." She turned back to the vendor quickly. "I don't suppose you take credit cards…?"

"I've got it," Max said from behind her. "And make it two."

Things inside her leaped at the close sound of his

voice. Danielle turned quickly to find him, and her heart stuttered a little. He looked incredible. He always looked incredible, but each time she saw him it struck her anew.

He was wearing jeans this time. Her own had been the right choice, then. Above the denim, he wore a navy-blue sports coat. He looked easy, relaxed, in his element, yet there was still that almost arrogant confidence, that edge. As she watched, he reached to the back pocket of his jeans, then he gave the vendor a ten-dollar bill.

Finally Danielle glanced up into his eyes. Pale blue, with that smile in them. This, she thought, was going to be a wonderful night, especially if she took care of the bird problem, to boot.

For the first time she realized that if she *did* manage to convince Senator Roberson to give up his land to-night, she would have no further excuse for wrangling with Maxwell. There would be no further need to entice him…except for the pure pleasure of it. There would be no more baseball stadiums. Danielle frowned.

Maxwell snapped his fingers in front of her eyes. Danielle blinked and came back quickly. "Thank you. I'm sorry—did you say something?"

"Just that I noticed you wandering around down here and figured you didn't know where to go. I thought I'd better intercept you." But that wasn't quite true, he realized. He *had* noticed her…but only because he'd been watching for her. Something about their telephone conversation yesterday morning had hinted to him that this might be a woman who didn't know a baseball from a hockey puck. That being the case, he'd surmised that she might not be familiar with the inside of a stadium. He'd kept an eye on the gate entrance—the one near the pickup window—so he could make sure she didn't get lost on her way to the sky box.

That was what he'd told himself he was doing. He hadn't been impatiently waiting for her to appear. His gaze hadn't *really* scoured every entrance in case she approached through one of the others instead. He would have preferred it if she wasn't coming to the game at all, if Stan had just condescended to hammering this out over the telephone. Then she'd arrived, and Max had found himself grinning at her obvious pleasure as she'd looked around the stadium.

"Nice cap, by the way," he said as he handed her one of the drinks.

She smiled at him. Her eyes were as bright as diamonds of sunlight dancing over a tropical sea of blue. Where had her glasses gone…and when had he ever gone poetic over a woman's eyes before?

Max's head began to swim.

"I'm partial to Jeff Gordon myself," he said, to say something.

"Jeff who?" she asked.

"Gordon. The Rainbow Warrior. He won NASCAR's Winston Cup a few years back. You're wearing his number there on your hat."

"Oh. Of course." She nodded and sipped her soft drink.

Then she stood on tiptoe to scan the stadium through the crowds passing in front of them. Her jacket was open, and when she stretched like that, the T-shirt she was wearing hiked up and showed a band of smooth skin at her waist. In a flash Max could almost feel it under his hands, like heated silk. The image was so vivid that he jolted, unsure for a wild moment if he'd actually touched her or not.

He'd been prepared to meet the woman in the sleek business suit with the stunning legs and long, manicured fingers. He'd even been hoping a little that the *other* Dani Harrington would show up—the one with the microscopic black skirt and the red lace. But this hint of skin at her waist threw him *way* off. How could she go from utterly professional to some kind of barefoot siren in red underwear to...to *this* in the matter of a week? She looked like a tomboy, wholesome and healthy, ready to either jump behind the wheel of a race car or wallop a ball out of the park—but equally enticing either way. Every time he encountered her, Max thought, some astounding new woman seemed to emerge from her depths.

"Visit our snack bar for one-dollar hot dogs in the first inning," she said suddenly.

"Huh?" Max gathered his wits again.

"That sign over there. It says hot dogs are only a dollar. They're less expensive than a soft drink? What an odd place this is."

"It's a promotion." Max dragged his gaze away from her waist. It didn't want to go. "So you like football, too? You're a Raiders fan." He gestured at the front of her T-shirt.

Danielle looked down. "Oh. Yes."

"You're a real sports connoisseuse." He wouldn't have guessed it, Max thought, not from their conversation yesterday. It was just another example of how she kept him off his stride and he didn't like it. "Let's go upstairs and enjoy the game. This way. There's an elevator next to the first concession stand. We'll take that."

Danielle started in that direction. Max didn't immediately move. His gaze sharpened on her as she moved ahead of him. Those jeans...He wasn't sure if a breath would fit between them and her skin.

It had been a bad, bad idea to join her and Stan here,

he thought again. This was not how a man went about keeping his distance. But Stan had been persistent, wouldn't let him off the hook. Max rubbed his jaw pensively, then he went after her.

In the elevator he hit the button for the sky box level. When the doors slid open again, she stepped out purposefully. "Which way?"

"Right there. The door that says Midland Construction."

"As in a company that could perhaps build a home on a vacant lot?" She sidestepped a group of chattering people heading in the opposite direction, then she stopped to look back at him. "Does Senator Roberson own Midland Construction?"

"He did the last time I checked. I take it your research into his business and personal holdings didn't extend that far."

She grinned. "Not yet."

He stepped closer to her, close enough to catch the misty scent of her perfume again. "You can stop digging now," he said quietly. "We'll finish this tonight."

His voice had gone husky again, Danielle thought. For a wild moment her mind went utterly blank. What, exactly, was he referring to? She'd been fine, she thought, until he'd moved close to her. He wore some kind of cologne that was both sharp and seductive, that was all male and so completely his style. It filled her head. She caught her breath because she wanted to inhale it deeply.

He was waiting for her to say something. "Will we?" she murmured.

How could a question be a promise? Max stepped back from her quickly. "If you let it happen."

Her breath caught. "I told you that I can be flexible. Try me."

Only if he lost his sanity entirely. "Stan isn't going to build on that land. And neither are you." Max reached over her shoulder to push open the door to the sky box.

"I believe that's still up for discussion."

"Are you going in?" he asked. "Or would you prefer that we stand here like this all night?"

Danielle stepped quickly into the sky box. "You never struck me as the sarcastic type."

"Maybe I get touchy when I'm cornered."

She wondered if he was referring to the plover mess…or something else. Something personal. His voice had taken on a new edge that for some reason had her heart skittering again. Danielle moved inside quickly, then she found herself face-to-face with Senator Stanley Roberson.

"Mrs. Harrington." He extended a hand to her.

Danielle took it. *This,* she thought, was ground she knew. "Senator." She paused to remove her baseball jacket, allowing him to take it from her. "It's a pleasure to meet you. But call me Danielle."

He nodded, still smiling. "I'm very glad you could join us. Are you a baseball fan?"

"Oh, certainly."

"And football and auto racing," Max interjected dryly.

"Someday we'll have to see about having you throw out the first pitch," Roberson said.

Throw a pitch? "Oh, no. I really prefer to stay out of the limelight."

The national anthem began playing. Danielle could hear it through speakers in each corner of the room, which was long and narrow with a small bar at one side. Opposite the bar was a seating area—a sofa, two chairs and a cocktail table. The far end of the room was all glass.

She went to the window and peered out. It was certainly an aerial view. She hugged herself, enjoying it.

"Would you care for something more to drink?" Max asked from behind her.

She uncrossed her arms and looked down at the paper cup in her hand. She'd drained the soft drink. "Yes. Please."

"Wine? Beer? Another soft drink?"

It happened so fast she nearly lost her breath. One moment she was intent on the field beneath her, then Maxwell's words penetrated. Beer? A memory of her father rolled over her with sweet nostalgia and ended with a painful tug at her heart. "A beer would be delightful." She had never had one in her life.

Max went to the refrigerator and snagged a bottle. That shadow had passed over her face again, he thought. He hadn't been entirely sure he'd seen it last Tuesday in her office, but this time he knew it had been real.

He didn't want her to have shadows, and he certainly didn't want to know what caused them. Somehow, that was worse than nearly invisible black skirts and red lace. It was worse than long, pretty fingers wrapping around a scotch glass as if they knew just how to encircle something. It was even worse than skin peeking out above the waist of her jeans.

He came out from behind the bar with a bottle and a glass. "You looked...lost for a minute there."

And now she looked startled. "I was just remembering something. My father used to sit in this big, brown leather recliner in our living room and as soon as the national anthem started playing on the television before a ball game, my mother would poke her head out of the kitchen to see if he wanted something to drink. She always said, *'Beer, Mike?'*"

"It sounds like a nice memory," Max murmured.

Danielle shook her head. Actually she wasn't sure that it was. A short time after that, her mother had given up her fight with cancer. It had happened on one of the many days when Michael Dempsey had been away, on the road. And there had never been any more beer in the house after that. They hadn't been home enough anymore for him to drink it.

"I don't need the glass." Danielle took the bottle from Max's hand and put it to her mouth. Her father had always upended it first, draining one long, satisfying swallow before nursing the rest. That, she thought, was how this should be done.

She decided she liked the almost-bitter smack of the beer challenging her taste buds.

Suddenly there was a roar through the speakers. The crowd outside the glass was going wild. She turned back in time to see the baseball sail over the wall at the far end of the field, and she clapped. "A home run!"

Max followed her gaze. "That's the wrong team. Our guys are the ones in black and silver." The woman hadn't the slightest clue about baseball, he realized. He'd been right the first time. The first baseman could probably throw a football to someone in the stands, and she wouldn't know anything was amiss.

What the hell was going on here?

Why would she try to convince him that she was an ardent fan? They weren't actually here to watch the game, anyway, so it wasn't as though he'd have to explain everything to her play by play.

Plovers, he thought. They were here to discuss birds and land. And it would be infinitely safer if he kept this conversation to business. "We've come up with a compromise," he said suddenly.

Danielle took her gaze from the field. "What sort of compromise?"

"Regarding your land."

One corner of her mouth curled into a smile. "Ah. That." She told herself she wasn't disappointed.

"What did you think I was talking about?"

"What else did you say we were here to discuss?" She paused, feigning thoughtfulness. "My name, I believe it was."

"And why you seem to think Danielle suits you."

She put the bottle to her mouth again. "It's who I am." But she remembered the sensation that had filled her downstairs, when she had looked at his strong handwriting scrawled across that envelope...and she wondered.

"Are you?" he asked.

"Maybe not," she said softly. "Maybe not always."

Business. What the hell was he talking about here?

"What's your proposal?" she asked.

To take you out of here and find out what kind of woman you are the rest of the time. "It's a counteroffer to the suggestion you made on the news Friday. Both you and Stan would donate your land as a refuge for the birds."

"Why would I want to do that?"

"There would be no need for your plover fund in this case. The money would, of course, revert back to you. You'd save yourself half a million dollars."

Her mind clicked back to business—easily, cleanly. It was firm ground. She was almost relieved. "My parcel cost me six hundred thousand. Actually, under your scenario, I wouldn't be able to develop it. I'd lose six hundred thousand, Senator, a tad more than the half-million extra I wouldn't have to spend.''

"But you'd gain immeasurable PR."

"With all due respect, I'm not sure I need PR. I'm not going to be running for reelection in three years." She shot an apologetic look at Stan. "I'd rather have the income from my resort—which, I might point out, should quickly surpass half a million—than have the county's population in awe of my altruistic gestures. Besides, I'm offering them jobs, tax dollars. As I also said on Friday, I believe they'll appreciate that more."

He'd been a fool to hope that that wouldn't occur to her, Max thought.

"Of course, if Roberson really feels the need to donate his parcel rather than have the fund purchase it," Danielle continued, "I'm sure your coalition could find some other use for the money. Didn't you say something about loons last week?"

"They're taken care of," he growled.

Danielle shrugged. "I only suggested that my fund pay for that land because I didn't realize how very generous the senator is." She glanced at Stan again and smiled. "I hope I didn't offend you."

She was good, Max thought. No matter that he fully intended to stop her in her tracks, no matter that she had him more confused than he'd been about any female since the age of sixteen—he had to appreciate her style.

Then she glanced his way and grinned wickedly. It was a gentle, sure, clever look capped by a wink, as though they shared a secret. It chopped his legs out from under him. Sort of like that come-hither glance over her shoulder on Friday, he thought...but worse.

"Maxwell?" she asked.

"What?" He realized—once again—that he hadn't

heard a single word she'd just said. Everything inside him started clamoring. *Run, get away from her, hurry.* He stood rooted, watching her.

"I wondered if I might have another of these beers. I won't be driving for a few more hours." When he didn't immediately respond, she leaned toward the bar to place her empty bottle there. And when she did, the T-shirt slid up her back. Skin peeked at him again, a good three or four inches of it this time.

There had to be a way to make her cooperate, but for the life of him Max couldn't think of it right now. He couldn't think of anything other than the way she'd feel beneath his hands.

Chapter Five

She'd won.

By the end of the ball game, it seemed obvious that there was nothing Maxwell would be able to do to stop her from breaking ground on the first of the month. She should feel jubilant, she thought as she watched the valet attendant approach with her car. But a feeling was starting to spread through her chest that she was all too familiar with, that achy, itchy sensation that came over her when all the rooms in her house were too quiet. Or in the supermarket line, on the rare trips she would make for something the housekeeper forgot, standing behind a mother with a squalling toddler, wishing she were that other woman with the heaped cart, despite the worried frown the woman wore as the cash register inched past a hundred dollars.

It was over now, just as Maxwell had predicted it would be before the game. But along with victory came the unnerving uncertainty that she was never going to feel the way she had these last couple of weeks again.

And somewhere in her heart she knew that that feeling had nothing to do with plovers.

Danielle pulled a bright smile from somewhere deep inside her as she slid behind the wheel of her car. "Thank you, Maxwell. That was fun…regardless of the outcome."

He bent so that he was peering in her window. His voice lowered a notch and took on that intimate huskiness she remembered from their telephone conversation yesterday. "I don't give up that easily."

Her heart clubbed her ribs. She wondered if he was talking about their feud…and she wished he was referring to something more personal. Danielle cocked a brow at him. "What can you possibly do now?"

"Why, Dani, are you asking me to tip my hand?" He grinned quickly. It was a flash of something rakish that made her nerve endings wake up.

"Of course I am. Forewarned is forearmed." She didn't bother to tell him not to call her Dani this time.

"I think I'll let you be surprised. Don't pout."

"I never pout." But if it had worked, she thought, she might have admitted to it.

He watched her face a moment longer. Danielle thought he might be about to say something else— maybe about seeing her again—and her heart jumped. But then he frowned. "Exactly how many beers did you have upstairs?"

"I'm fine," she said quietly, feeling deflated.

"How many?" he persisted.

She'd only had the two, and that had been a few hours ago. But until she knew where he was going with this, she decided to keep that to herself. "Why?"

"Your cheeks are all rosy. Your eyes are too bright."

It was possible that that was the result of moment after moment spent in his company, she thought. She'd never quite admitted that all she knew about baseball was that her father had enjoyed it. But once it had become clear that she wasn't going to budge on the absurd issue of donating her land, Max had given way to explaining the finer points of the game. She'd watched his expression grow animated, and one time he'd actually put his hand on her shoulder to lean forward and point down to the field.

Then he'd snatched it back again as though she had scalded him.

Danielle wasn't sure what that had been about. She didn't think he considered her distasteful, not after the way he'd been looking at her on that video tape. It had left her feeling edgy, expectant and confused.

Now he straightened from the car and rapped his fist gently against her roof. He seemed agitated.

"What?" Danielle asked. "What is it?"

What it was, Max thought, was that he couldn't let her drive.

He couldn't get in that car with her, either. He knew his limits, and he'd reached one about forty-five minutes ago when Lenny Hager had hit into a triple play and he'd found himself touching her, just a hand on her shoulder, but damn it, he'd been relaxed, enjoying himself, enjoying her, and it had felt like the most natural thing in the world. Add to that the glimpse of skin above the waistband of her jeans, to that quick shadow that could pass over her eyes at times, and Max knew the best thing—the only thing—he could do for himself tonight was get into his own Jeep and drive like hell, as far and as fast away from her as possible.

Then he heard his own voice say, "Move over."

"I beg your pardon?" Her voice had a pitch to it that said she had no idea what he was talking about.

"I'm driving you home." He opened her car door.

"I can't move over."

"Why not?" he growled, not the least bit comfortable with the circumstances that had led to this decision. And maybe just a little too happy. He wasn't sure which bothered him more.

"There's a gear shift between my seat and the passenger side," she explained.

"Then climb over it!" But, of course, a woman like her wouldn't climb, he thought. Or would she? Danielle wouldn't. Dani might. "Or get out and walk around," he continued. "Damn it, this shouldn't be so difficult."

"But it is."

"Why?" He knew he fairly snarled the word.

"Because one might presume that you arrived here in a vehicle of your own."

Danielle heard her own voice and winced. *Professional.* What had Angelique called it? Professional *ice.* She wanted this. She wanted more time with him before it was over. She wanted it so much that she unconsciously fell back onto everything she was familiar with, all the ground she knew. Logic. Facts. Common sense. She was safe with that. "If you drive me home," she pointed out, "then your car will still be here. And how will you get from my house to yours?"

She wasn't prepared for his reaction. Somehow her elbow ended up in his hand and the next thing she knew she was outside her car, her spine pressed against the low roof, her jaw hanging in surprise. And his face was very, very close to hers.

Her heart started drumming. She waited. He didn't move.

"Fine," he said softly, finally. "Point taken. We'll leave your *vehicle* here and take mine. I'll drop you off, then I'll go home."

"More's the pity." Danielle felt her face flame with even more color. *Where had that come from?*

It had come from the fact that his mouth was still inches from hers. Because she thought she could taste him already, and everything coiled tight inside her with anticipation. Her nerve endings thrummed. She hadn't known they could do that.

Then Max reared back. "You don't know what you're saying."

That insulted her. Maybe because it was close to true. "I'm thirty-six years old. I have an idea."

No, he thought, she didn't. Because she had been married to a man who loved her and who had died before that feeling could wane. Max stepped back from her car. "Get in."

Expectancy drained out of her, leaving her feeling as if her limbs had filled with air. "Get *in?* You wanted me out, now you want me in?"

"I'll follow you home to make sure you're safe." The truth of the matter was that *she* seemed a whole lot steadier right now than he was.

More's the pity. The invitation had had a certain lilt that touched something very, very deep in his soul. And that scared the hell out of him. It brought a panic as old as his memories and just as painful. He closed his eyes, trying to get a grip on himself.

She wasn't going to move on the land issue. Other than Stan's injunction, he had nothing else up his sleeve. It was over. This was what he had wanted. He wouldn't have to cross paths with her again.

He would dredge up a date tomorrow night, go out

with someone seductive and easy who had no expectations, and he would put Dani Harrington out of his mind.

Her car door cracked shut again with such force his eyes flew open again.

"Don't bother," she said flatly.

Had she imagined it, that heartbeat of time when he'd seemed on the verge of kissing her? When maybe he would take her outrageous invitation in hand—so to speak—and drag her closer? Danielle put the BMW in gear hard and gunned the engine, then she drove out of the parking lot.

Oh, yes, she had a lot to learn about men.

Max hurried back to his Jeep, which the valet attendant had pulled up behind hers. He dove behind the wheel and took off after her. She drove straighter than a rookie out of the police academy trying to prove his worth. He followed her along the coastal highway.

Then he turned off toward the beach while she headed inland toward the estate he knew she'd once shared with Richard Harrington. For the first time he wondered just what she did inside that place all alone. His thoughts veered toward things like a bubbling Jacuzzi with her inside it...naked. Everything came to life inside him all over again.

Ruthlessly he brought his mind back to driving. When Stan got that injunction in place, it was going to serve a double purpose, he decided again. It would stop her from developing that land and it would ensure that he didn't cross paths with her even one more time. He felt a spasm of regret in his stomach. He enjoyed her reactions and that quicksilver mind of hers. But she did things to him that he just didn't want done.

He'd damned near *kissed* her, he thought. There had been a sweet and anticipatory hunger in her expression, no more come-hither smiles, no more saucy and intimate winks. And *that* made the urge to lower his mouth to hers even more treacherous. He wasn't sure if he'd ever felt that way and he'd wanted to share it with her...for just a moment.

With that thought, Max missed his next turn. He dragged on the wheel and cut a U-turn, then he headed toward his own town house. It was on the beach, but he hadn't displaced any wildlife to own here. The only birds that visited his land were a few gulls now and then. Max drove into his carport, got out of his Jeep and stood on the concrete. He frowned to himself, his keys in his hand. Then, instead of looking down toward the churning sea as he usually did, he found himself turning in the opposite direction, staring up at the hills and the twinkling lights of the homes there.

He wondered which was hers. There were several clinging to the hillsides, palatial, majestic...anyone of them would have suited her.

Now he was *dwelling* on her.

Fear rushed into his blood again. With a single frantic pump of his heart, something clammy poured through his whole body. He was in trouble, he thought. He had to resolve this bird issue. Quickly. Before he completely lost his mind.

"What's this?" Danielle stood from her desk on Wednesday morning as a man entered her office with Angelique. Unless she badly missed her guess, he was some kind of court officer. He had that look about him. And Angelique appeared angry.

"He insisted that he had to see you personally," Angelique said tightly. "I couldn't stop him."

Bingo. Something seemed to chime in Danielle's

head. The man was holding papers. She smiled to herself. On to round two, she thought, delighted. After last night she'd been sure their war was over. But Maxwell *had* had something else up his sleeve. Whatever this was, it would almost certainly mean that they would have to meet again.

She came around her desk to meet the man. "That's fine. What can I do for you?"

"I just need you to sign this acknowledgment of service."

"Certainly." Danielle scrawled her name quickly, took the papers and scanned them. Then her heart plunged.

An *injunction?*

He'd found a sympathetic judge who was disallowing her from breaking ground on the first of the month! "Call the legal department," she said to Angelique even as she tried to get her breath back. She felt as though someone had punched her. "I want to meet with them ASAP."

Angelique hurried off, and Danielle shook the papers in the man's face. "This was sneaky!"

He took a quick step back. "I wouldn't know, ma'am."

"He did it behind my back! He didn't even talk to me about it!" And that, she knew, was what bothered her. He'd done it without even warning her!

The court officer beat a hasty retreat, and Danielle went back to her desk. She sat hard in her chair. So this was the flip side of that zing and wallop of hormones, she thought, biting her lip. There was a sharp sensation in the area of her chest. It felt like betrayal.

Her intercom rang. Danielle snatched up the phone. "Yes?"

"Mr. Becker, Mr. Miller and Mr. Bruso are waiting for you in the conference room," Angelique said.

Her legal team. "Never mind," Danielle said suddenly, changing gears. If he thought he could just slide this in on her blindly, she decided, then Maxwell Padgett had a thing or two to learn about his opponent.

Danielle left her office, the papers still clutched in her hand. She marched right past Angelique with her purse slung over her shoulder.

"You're leaving?" Angelique gaped at her. *"Again?"*

Danielle set her jaw. "I most certainly am."

Max sat at his desk, his feet up on the wood, the phone to his ear. He told himself that it was relief that had him feeling empty and dull. "It's in your hands now," he told Stan. "I'm out of it. I punched the injunction through, now go present some legislation."

"She can fight back," Stan warned.

"Of course she can. And she will." But that, Max thought, would take place in a courtroom into which he had no intention of setting foot.

He wouldn't have to see her again. And that was a good thing, he reminded himself. She would be safely removed from his life before he could do something utterly insane like give in to that compulsion to touch his mouth to hers.

She chose that moment to sail into his office.

Max's heart stalled, and he lost his air. Her hair was windblown and her eyes were alive. Her skirt was longer than the one she'd worn at the beach, shorter than the one he'd encountered her in that first night in her office when she'd sat in her chair and crossed one elegant leg coolly over the other. She wore steep black heels and a sweater that was cut just low enough at the neck that he had a hard time looking anywhere else.

Max hung up on Stan in midsentence.

He thought fast while he brought his feet down from his desk. "Running around topless again?"

The question had the effect he'd intended. Danielle froze halfway to his desk...a safe distance away. As long as she wasn't close enough to touch, he would be fine, he told himself.

"What?" she gasped in response to his question.

He circled a finger at his own head. "Your hair is all messy. You must have had the top down on your car."

"What does that have to do with anything?"

"It was just an observation." *To keep you on that side of the room.*

Danielle smoothed a hand over her hair. *He'd noticed her appearance.* Maybe she wasn't an expert in these things, but it seemed to her that if he was noticing her hair, then he wasn't as immune to her as he'd seemed last night. "I gave you more credit," she said finally, bringing her dazed mind back to what he had done.

One brow climbed Maxwell's forehead. "You knew I was going to keep fighting you."

"I thought you'd do it head-on, not take this kind of cowardly approach."

That brought him to his feet with a scowl. She moved toward his desk again, but he held a hand out to stop her. "Stay put," he said quickly.

Danielle frowned and looked behind her, at the spot on the carpet where she had just been standing. Then something sizzled through her mind, a certainty that made her heart leap. She had no idea how she knew or why she was so sure, but she was. *She made him nervous.*

Call it female intuition—something she'd never known she possessed before—but he was *fighting* his attraction to her, Danielle thought. She remembered the way he had pulled his hand back fast when he'd put it on her shoulder last night. The way he had almost kissed her...only to grow angry. Now he had mentioned her hair, and he was as high-strung and skittish as a race-horse.

He didn't even want her to take another step closer to him.

"Are you suggesting that I stand back there?" she asked. "Where I was?"

"Yes." His voice dropped a notch into that low growl again.

"I can't sit down?"

"No."

"Why not?"

"You won't be staying that long."

"But I'm in no rush." She looked back at him in time to see him rub his forehead as though he had a headache. Danielle proceeded to the chair in front of his desk and she sat down. It gave her an exhilarating, heady thrill when he frowned and backed up quickly to stand behind his own chair.

"You came into my office uninvited last Tuesday," she reminded him, then she leaned forward to rest her elbows provocatively on his desk. "Now we're even."

"We were even when you came storming in here two minutes ago without knocking. Now you're one up on me."

Danielle nodded. "True. Okay, feel free to pay me back at some future time."

"No need. I'll let you win this particular round."

"Is something wrong?"

"No," he said too quickly. "Why?"

"You just managed a pretty clever—albeit dastardly—coup." She straightened again and crossed her legs. "I thought you'd be more triumphant, less cranky."

Max felt his gaze tug to her legs. He pulled it back again.

"You won't even discuss this?" she asked.

"You're barking up the wrong tree." Max moved to his window and yanked up the blinds, looking out, looking anywhere but at her. "I have no part in this any longer."

"Of course you do."

"I do not."

"Your coalition got the injunction. You can withdraw it."

Is that what it will take to make you go away? Max almost said it aloud and was appalled at himself. He'd almost—*almost*—considered sacrificing umpteen untold plovers in an effort to save his own hide from something he was wanting more and more the longer she remained in his office.

He caught her scent again, that gentle, clingy, misty fragrance he'd first noticed at the beach site. Damn it, he had to get her out of here.

"I'm not going to withdraw it," he said. "So go harass Stan."

"I'd rather fight with you."

He glanced her way again sharply. A mistake. She recrossed her legs again slowly. Was she doing that on *purpose?* It wasn't possible, he decided. She wasn't that cruel. His mouth went dry all the same, and something kicked at his chest from the inside. He thought it might be his heart.

"I'm not going to fight," he said hoarsely. "I can let the lawyers and the politicians take it from here."

"But you won't."

Max chose to misunderstand. "It's a perfectly legal move," he said, nodding at the papers she held.

"Why didn't you call me?" she countered. "Shouldn't I have been at this mockery of a court hearing?"

"You don't need an actual hearing to get an injunction. And you don't have to notify the other side."

"That's un-American. How can a judge stop me without even hearing my side of it?"

"Because there will be time for everyone to tell their sides later. All I did was convince a judge that we need more time for legal remedies to be pursued. This isn't so much a ruling as it is a pause, Dani. The judge isn't stopping you. He's just saying you can't move ahead at this particular point in time. He's freezing a contentious situation until it can be resolved."

"There's nothing to resolve," she reminded him. "I'm totally permitted." Then she understood and she felt her head go light. "Senator Roberson is going to use this time to inspire new legislation, isn't he? That could take *years!*"

"I hope so."

But even if Roberson somehow got legislation through, Danielle thought, she had an excellent argument for grandfathering her permits in. She finally stood. "Then I guess I'll see you in court." She turned for the door.

Max forced himself to move back to his desk. "Not me. Stan's lawyers."

"Ah, I forgot that part."

Roger Kimmelman chose that moment to step into the

room. Max thought the man looked remarkably unruffled given that the woman he considered to be their archenemy was standing no more than three feet from him.

"Why not you?" Roger asked Max, catching the end of their conversation. "You always—"

Max glared him into silence.

Roger frowned. "Ms. Harrington, your secretary just called. No emergency. She just wanted to know if this was where you had gone and when she might expect you back. Apparently, your legal team is asking for you."

"Could you please tell her that I'm on my way back now?"

"Sure. Sure, of course. Ah…what was her name again? Angela?"

"Angelique," Danielle replied absently.

"Right. I'll take care of it." He retreated from the room.

Max frowned after him. He was so busy wondering what was wrong with his aide that he completely missed it when Danielle stepped up to his desk again. He jerked his gaze away from the door and she was…there, right there, her mouth inches from his again as she leaned toward him. His gaze dropped to her lips, and his heart kicked again.

"Thanks for your time," she said softly, then she retreated.

Max watched her step through the door, then he pulled his chair out and sat hard, blowing his breath out. For the first time in his life he knew what quicksand felt like.

Danielle was halfway back to her office before she thought to question what she had just accomplished.

There was still an injunction against her site, and it was going to take some time to remove it. She might miss the date targeted for her groundbreaking, and every day's delay after that would begin costing her money. Certain workers had contracts—they would have to be paid whether they were actually building anything out there or not.

But, she thought, *but...* Maxwell Padgett was rattled by her. So all she had to do now was keep the ball rolling long enough to maintain contact between them. Then it came to her—the perfect solution. Danielle turned up the radio and hummed along with the music as she drove, feeling a sweet kind of high.

When she got back to her office, she parked in the underground garage and rode the elevator up to the penthouse floor. Angelique was grinning at a spot on the wall. Danielle frowned at her vacant expression, then she waved a hand in front of her secretary's eyes.

"I'm back," she said.

"Oh." Angelique blinked at her. "The lawyers are preparing some sort of response and they want to confer with you."

"I'll meet them in the conference room, but I need you to do me a favor while I'm tied up there. Find out who owns the land on the other side of mine from the senator's."

"The other side?" Angelique frowned. "Why?"

"I'm going to buy it."

Chapter Six

Two days later Danielle stood at her office window, looking out. Black-gray clouds shifted and rolled across the sky the way they had the first time Maxwell had surprised her here. But this time she was expecting him.

She'd just spent seven hundred and fifty thousand dollars on more Gold Beach land, she thought dazedly. Coupled with the half million she'd already thrown at the plovers, she was up to her financial ears in this mess. It was preposterous. True, Richard's dying wish had been that she should use his money in whatever way made her happiest…as long as she didn't let the corporation and those funds flounder. But what would he say if he knew that she was doing this because of another man?

The other explanation was even worse—that she was doing it as a matter of pride and stubbornness. And she knew, deep in her heart, that both were true. When had this stopped being about Harrington Enterprises and become all about *her*?

Danielle shivered a little as though the chill outside her window had reached through the glass to touch her skin. Somewhere along the line, she thought, during these crazy and provocative past weeks, she'd stopped caring about the financial bottom line where her new resort was concerned. She had started flirting with Maxwell because it was fun, and because it was a way to win the right to develop her resort free of his interference. But then…then everything had changed.

It had become a matter of not losing him, of keeping him in her life. And it had become a matter of her dreams.

Danielle sighed. She knew better than to build this resort at any cost. Richard had taught her well, and she knew that at some point her investment would exceed any acceptable reward. She'd earn her money back eventually, but if she spent so much that it didn't happen for eight or nine more years, then—no—that was not a wise business decision. But she wanted this resort on that particular stretch of sand. And she wanted the man who was trying to stop her. So she was willing to push the issue up against any outrageous wall.

"What the holy hell do you think you're doing? Are you out of your mind?"

Danielle turned quickly away from the window. Maxwell entered her office the same way he had before, with a step as quiet as snow falling. But this time his voice had a bite to it.

He held papers in his hand. A quick glance told her they were probably copies of her closing documents. She'd paid cash for the adjoining land on the other side of her parcel, and that had enabled her to seal the deal this afternoon. There had been no doubt in her mind that once Maxwell found out about her purchase, she would be seeing him.

"Well," Danielle said, "I guess this makes us just about even again."

"'Even'? *I* haven't been running around spending millions of dollars trying to win this contest of wills!"

She winced a little at that and hoped he didn't notice. "I was referring to our habit of barging into each other's offices."

She'd flinched, he thought. Why? Had he struck a nerve? He lowered his voice to a growl. "This makes literally no financial sense."

"I know it."

She turned to the window again quickly, giving him her back. But just before she did, he saw it again, that deep frown pulling at her brow, the shadow moving in her eyes. Damn it, she was throwing him off by being vulnerable. And what was she doing by admitting that she was ignoring the bottom line? He wanted to stay angry. Instead, he felt something almost tender begin to fill his chest.

"It's very important to me to build there," she said finally.

He didn't want to know, and he heard himself ask, "Why?"

She turned back to face him again. "Would you care for a drink?"

"Rather than an answer?"

"I'm offering one and not the other. I'm not sure you have a choice."

He decided to let her slide on it. For now. "Scotch?"

She nodded. "It can be our little tradition for bird fights in my office."

"Fine, then."

He watched her make the drinks. This time she poured them an equal measure. Somehow that alarmed him more than what she had done the last time.

"I'll answer your question if you answer one of mine," she said finally, carrying their glasses toward him.

Max eased back to sit against the edge of her desk. He accepted his own. "I'll reserve judgment until I hear what yours is."

She sipped. "Why do I make you nervous?"

He'd already taken a mouthful, and he choked on it. "Who said you did?"

Danielle wondered how far she could trust her instincts. Businesswise, they were honed. But as far as this male-female sort of thing was concerned, she was a babe in the woods. Still, she'd always believed that a well-placed gamble could pay off now and again. She went around her desk and sat in her chair. "You seem pretty intent on keeping an arm's length between us."

"Business is between us."

She noticed that he was swigging down his own drink pretty quickly. He finally sat, as well, in the chair opposite her desk.

"Was business why you pulled me out of my car the other night?"

"That was just common sense. I thought you'd had more to drink than you'd had."

Danielle finally nodded. "My mistake, then."

"Speaking of business, so is a million-three plus change in unanswered money. That's a lot of investment."

Danielle shrugged, but it felt brittle. "In case you missed the news coverage, I have it to burn."

He'd never paid much attention to the details, Maxwell thought. He just knew that Richard Harrington had left her loaded, and, of course, she must have earned a hefty salary for running the corporation. His eyes narrowed on her face. "So what do you do with all of it?" he heard himself ask.

She gave a quick peal of tense laughter. "Just lately I've been fighting birds."

"Besides that."

She seemed to think about it. "Would you believe me if I told you that it was just there?" she asked, looking down into her drink. "Until these last few days, I never had too much to do with it. It keeps accumulating on its own because I rarely spend it, except on the usual things, the mortgage and the car."

That startled him. "You run this place." He waved a hand at her office.

She looked up quickly. "Oh, but that's different. That's corporate money. I thought we were talking about my own."

So there was a delineation there, Max thought. Interesting.

"I get up in the morning, I come to work, I go home. I just live. I never see the bills and I never do anything particularly extravagant."

"Except buy land that you don't need."

"There is that." She paused, almost smiling. "In a respect, your little plovers have changed my life."

"I'll be sure to mention it to them while they slowly go extinct."

"It might be wiser to explain to them the virtues of sharing. In the meantime, I guess I'll just keep throwing money at the problem. It's fun to be reckless once in a while."

Reckless? That brought to mind images that he definitely did not want to entertain. Too many of them involved her in a bed. Max cleared his throat. "So what are you going to do with this latest purchase?"

Her blue eyes snapped back to full alert. "Oh, no, you don't. You never answered *my* question. We were going to exchange, remember?"

"You said that. I didn't." He leaned back in his chair and sipped scotch, determined to appear nonchalant.

"Clever." Her laughter came then, and it rippled over his skin. Max wondered if he had lost his mind, to be sitting here with her, talking like this over good scotch.

"Besides," he continued, "my original question wasn't about what you're going to do with the land you bought today. It was why is it so important to you to build your resort right there on Gold Beach. Why not somewhere else?"

How could he do that with his voice? she wondered dazedly. He made it dip so it sounded smoky and private. Like they were the only two people left in the world and he knew every secret inside her. It almost made her forget that he was trying to slide into parts of her heart that she never shared.

Then he met her eyes and held them. It was a moment in which the air in the room seemed to evaporate. What was left in the vacuum was heat. Her heart started galloping. Yes, she thought, yes, there was definitely something going on between them. She didn't need to be a femme fatale to feel this.

She reached quickly and set her glass on her desk. As triumphantly female as she'd felt in his office two days ago, now she felt shaken to the core. She didn't know what to do next.

"There are a few issues I need to work out yet regarding the new land,'' she said quickly, and, she realized, a little hoarsely.

''Such as?''

''I'm not ready to divulge them yet.'' She had no clue whatsoever what they might be.

The ink wasn't even dry on her closing papers yet. All she knew for sure was that she'd bought that parcel so as not to lose touch with this man and now, suddenly, she didn't care about sidetracking him anymore at all. Because if she made him forget about the plovers, if he gave up and she didn't see him again, it would leave something painfully hollow inside her.

She'd be back to feeling the way she had before he'd come into her life.

''How do you do that?'' he asked suddenly.

Danielle frowned. ''Do what?''

''Go from sultry to CEO in the blink of an eye. Is this another Dani/Danielle thing? Which is real? The corporate warrior or the woman inside?''

Danielle shook her head a little. *Sultry?* Her? She couldn't focus. It was all she could do not to jump and check her reflection in the window glass.

''You're not answering,'' he prompted her.

How could she tell him that the change came over her whenever she felt out of her depth with him, terrified and titillated and alive? ''I'll call you in two days,'' she said quickly. ''I'll bring you up to speed on my plans.''

''Two days,'' he repeated, draining his scotch. ''I'll be waiting.''

A shiver rolled through her again, from the top of her head down to the bottom of her toes.

Max stood. She watched him go.

When she heard his footsteps recede down the hallway, Danielle finally jolted to her feet. She hurried to her office door and peered out. It was late, past six, and Angelique's desk was vacant. Danielle jogged into the main hallway and looked at the lit numbers above the elevator doors. Maxwell was halfway down to the garage.

Good enough.

Danielle tore up the hallway, looking for any lit office she could find. She didn't have the luxury of waiting for opportunity to fall into her lap this time. She needed help *now*.

Morris Becker, the head of her legal department, was still at his desk.

"Hi," she said, stepping breathlessly into his office.

He looked up at her, startled. "Ms. Harrington. I'm sorry. I thought we told you. The judge won't decide on our own petition until at least Monday."

Danielle waved a hand. She scarcely cared. "I'm not here to bother you about that. I know you're doing all you can." If worse came to worst, she thought, she always had the new land. It would take some time to get everything repermitted, but it was an option.

Becker looked confused. "What then?"

What was his wife's name? "Millie."

"You want to talk to me about Millie?" His frown furrowed his forehead even more deeply.

"Actually, I wanted to ask you something."

He sat back in his chair like a man resigned to a firing squad. "Go right ahead."

"How long have you been married?"

"Thirty-six years in June."

That, Danielle thought, was a lot of marriage. "What made it last? No, no." She shook her head quickly. "I don't mean what made it last thirty-six years. I meant…how did you…get past the first date? Those first months, what kept you coming back for more?''

"More?'' She thought he was about to choke.

"More of Millie's company.''

"You're asking me to remember back thirty-six years?''

Danielle hesitated. "Yes. If you could?''

Becker finally shook his head, but then he smiled to himself. "You know, if you hadn't mentioned it, I might have forgotten. But it was her cooking. Millie has always been a wonderful cook. In those early days she used to invite me to dinner.''

"Dinner,'' Danielle echoed. Oh, this was not good. All she knew about dinner was that her housekeeper made it.

"Yes.'' He chuckled. "I guess it's true that the way to a man's heart is through his stomach. Why do you ask?''

Danielle shook her head quickly and backed toward the door. "I was just curious.''

"Well, then.'' Becker cleared his throat. He looked grim and determined. "As long as we're being honest, I'd like to mention something. Of course, if I'm out of line—''

"Then I'll tell you,'' Danielle said. She knew what was coming.

"You have the board very alarmed, Ms. Harrington, with this latest acquisition. They're concerned by your behavior.'' And his eyes said that this visit she'd just made to him wasn't helping matters any.

"I'll take it under advisement. Thank you for your concern.'' Danielle turned to go.

"Ms. Harrington, is everything all right with you…ah, personally?''

It stopped her at the door. "Everything is fine, Mr. Becker." She stepped out into the hall again and closed his door quietly behind her. Then her heart plunged.

Dinner?

Max leaned one elbow on the bar and watched the senator approach through the happy-hour haze of smoke, people and voices. His best friend didn't look happy.

"Is there a reason we're doing this here instead of my nice, quiet rec room?" Stan asked when he reached him.

Max nodded and swallowed another mouthful of scotch. "Yes. Marcy."

"You've suddenly decided you don't like my fiancée?" Stan looked dumbfounded—and angry. "I've got to tell you, Max, your reaction to my wedding plans is a little extreme. And it could drive the first wedge into a twenty-plus-year friendship."

There, Max thought. There was a prime example of how terrible and terrifying this whole issue of women could be. They could actually make a man threaten to turn his back on his closest friend. Max held up a hand. "I like Marcy. I've always liked Marcy."

"But?" Stan prompted.

"But I wanted you to be able to talk without her overhearing."

"There's nothing I can say to you that I can't say to her."

"Are you serious?" That staggered him a little, too.

"Of course, I am"

Max was suddenly wary. "Does that work both ways? Do you tell her things I tell you?"

Stan scowled. "Not unless you give me the go-ahead."

"Well, I'm not giving it."

Stan looked at him oddly. "Okay. What's on your mind?"

Max was somewhat mollified. "Dani Harrington bought the land on the *other* side of her parcel today. For seven hundred and fifty thousand dollars."

Stan nearly fell off his bar stool. "Is she crazy? It's not worth that much."

"It is when you want it fast and without a hassle."

"What's she going to do, put *that* aside for the birds, too? Put a towering Harrington resort right in the middle of it all?"

"I don't know what she's up to." Max paused. "I was hoping you could tell me."

Stan's drink came, and he downed a mouthful. "I barely know her. I only met her that one night at the ballpark. How would I know? You talk to her more often than I do."

"But you know women."

Stan looked startled, then he laughed. "You're finally admitting I have an edge over you there?"

"Not likely. But you're about to go marrying one, so maybe you have some secret insight that I don't. That's all I'm conceding."

"Are you asking specifically about Danielle Harrington?"

Max squirmed inwardly. "This is between us, right?" he asked again.

"If you say so."

"Okay, then. When she was talking to me about that new land tonight…she looked at me."

"She looked at you," Stan repeated.

"For a long time."

"Was she in the same room with you?"

"Yes. Of course she was."

"Well, then, that makes sense."

Max was frustrated. He tried a different avenue. "Do you think a woman would spend three-quarters of a million dollars just because she thought she made a man...I don't know, nervous?"

Stan laughed. "Sure, if she had it. So? Does she make you nervous?"

Max scowled fiercely. "Why should she?"

"Because she has an immediate and overwhelming effect on you that you can't explain."

"She does not."

"Hey, friend, I saw that television tape the day she confronted you on Gold Beach. You were hyperventilating."

Max opened his mouth to deny it and couldn't.

"So what does my Marcy have to do with any of this?" Stan asked.

"When you met her, did she have an immediate and overwhelming effect on you that you couldn't explain?" Max almost didn't want to know. "She's not here, so you can be honest."

"It wouldn't matter. She already knows. When I met her, it took me a day and a half to remember how to breathe again."

Max grimaced. "Still, you didn't think about marrying her until now."

"Of course not. It scared the hell out of me."

Max gave thanks for small miracles. His friend was still somewhat sane after all. "Getting married or not breathing?" he asked, just to be sure.

"Both."

Even more sensible, Max thought. He pushed his edge. "But you're doing it. You're marrying her. You didn't avoid her."

She wouldn't let me.'' Stan polished off his drink.

Max's heart sank. "I think I've got a problem.''

"Well,'' Stan said, ever the politician, "just don't go soft on her until you manage to get all that land away from her. *Two* parcels now? Whoa.''

"I keep telling you, I'm out of it.''

"You were out of it until she dropped seven hundred and fifty thousand bucks on a new lot. Now you're back in.''

That, Max thought, was what he had been afraid of.

"I'm going home to Marcy,'' Stan said.

"See you later.'' Max barely looked up from his drink. His mind rolled back to that intense, sultry gaze in her office that had held his for far too many moments to be comfortable. Oh, yes, he thought, he was back in. And if she called him in two days, then he only had limited time to decide what he was going to do about it.

Chapter Seven

The following morning at half past eleven, Danielle took a deep breath and picked up the telephone. She called the coalition. It was Saturday, but she thought he might be there, anyway.

A man with a forceful, urgent voice answered the line. She thought it might be Maxwell's aide, the one she had met in his office several days ago. When she asked for Maxwell, he wanted to know who was calling.

"Danielle—" She broke off. No, she thought, not Danielle.

Danielle would be following her head, not her heart, where this land was concerned. Danielle's world was silent, filled with her own company. Danielle had never lost her breath over a stare.

"It's Dani Harrington," she said finally.

There was a pause, a click, then Maxwell's voice filled the line. "Buy any more land lately?"

It happened the way it always did, that kick of her heart when he greeted her. But now, she thought, there was something else, too. She felt a smile pull at her mouth at his humor. "Ah, no," she replied. She still wasn't even sure what she was going to do with what she already had. But if he accepted the offer she was about to make, then she figured she had forty-eight more hours or so to come up with something.

"Glad to hear it." His voice shared secrets again. "I'm running out of brilliant countermoves."

"Somehow I doubt that."

"Why, Dani, was that a compliment?"

"I figured I owed you one after that *sultry* comment you made."

He wondered if she didn't know that about herself. He didn't think she did. "Then I'll take it. But my guess is that you didn't call to discuss compliments."

"No. Plovers."

"I'm always willing to listen to anything you have to say."

"I was thinking more along the lines of…in person."

His silence was so long Dani felt her heart flop over. Was she being too forward, too aggressive? She should have checked this out with Angelique first. Then she rallied.

"Getting nervous again?"

"That's some kind of imagination you have."

"I have many talents."

"Hmm. You have provocation down to an art."

Dani lost her breath for a moment. Well, she had always believed that practice made perfect. "And generosity. I'm willing to give you one more chance to try to change my mind about the land."

"That's a difficult offer to turn down."

"Then don't." Dani rushed on before she lost the last

of her nerve. "My house. Monday night at seven. I'll even feed you."

"There's no need—"

"See you then." She hung up, practically slamming the phone down before he could finish. Then she rubbed her damp palms on her skirt. She picked up the telephone and called her housekeeper. "Mrs. Dunley, I'm going to need some help."

Maxwell turned into her long, meandering driveway just after seven o'clock on Monday night. He was fashionably late. He had an idea that that sort of thing mattered in homes such as this.

He shouldn't be here, he thought. It was insanity. She wasn't going to change her mind about developing Gold Beach. Women who were going to change their minds didn't drop three-quarters of a million dollars on more land.

He told himself that he was only here because she'd hung up too quickly. She'd never given him the chance to politely decline her offer. She'd disconnected before he could suggest an alternate place to meet. He'd had no choice to but accept her invitation.

He'd had two days to call her back.

Max finally got out of his Jeep. He hesitated a minute, trying to remember how to breathe.

He kept his hands deep in his pockets as he stared at the house. He looked up at the massive walls of red brick, at the ivory pillars bracketing her door. Beyond it, land dove off into nowhere; just as he had imagined, the house clung to the side of the old Beach Hills. The place didn't suit her at all, he thought, though three weeks ago he might have thought so. In fact, the woman who'd first met him in her office, the one with the very nice legs and the cunning to try to make his drink stronger than her own, was one who would probably be at home here. But he couldn't picture the NASCAR-football-baseball fan striding through these hallowed halls. As for the woman in red lace, well…his mind leaped to an image of a Jacuzzi again.

He damned well ought to get right back in his Jeep and go home.

He could call her on his cell phone and offer profuse apologies, Max thought, maybe make an excuse about an unexpected meeting. He found himself moving toward her door instead. The hand he lifted to the big brass knocker might well have belonged to someone else.

He knocked once, twice, then a third time. Nothing happened. *He'd gotten a reprieve.*

He waited for the relief to come. Instead, his heart rate accelerated. She'd been hurt, had smashed up that little green car of hers on some highway somewhere, and of course no one would think to notify him. Then temper blindsided him, hot and pulsing behind his eyes. She'd changed her mind, hadn't even bothered to call and tell him.

Except he knew in his gut that that wasn't her style at all. Even without being a polished CEO, she was kind, almost innocent when she wasn't being perceptive, provocative and cutthroat. She was honest. She wouldn't stand him up. Something else was wrong then, something—

She opened the door, and Max felt his jaw sag.

This time she wore a short blue jumper over a white ribbed turtleneck…and oven mitts on her hands. She was barefoot again. One lock of dark hair had escaped from being tucked behind her ear. It obscured one clear blue eye. As he stared, she took a deep breath and blew it away.

"You're late," she said.

Max closed his mouth. "Are you all right?"

A frown creased her forehead. "Of course I'm all right. Don't I look all right?"

"Frankly...I don't know." He had no idea what "all right" was supposed to look like on this particular woman. Tonight she was Betty Crocker. "All right" for Betty Crocker was probably a lot different from "all right" for a NASCAR fan. "You seem harried," he said finally.

She stepped back from the door and waved him inside. "Not at all. I'm in my element."

"Okay." Max stepped past her.

Whatever else he'd been about to say died in his throat as he entered the wide main hall of her home. It was staggering. There was a black-and-white marble floor that was larger than many small countries. He tilted his head back and looked up. The ceiling was opened to the next floor. A gleaming mahogany balustrade lined the corridor up there. The staircase swept down, right to left, curving. Various ferns and plants—some taller than he was—were placed strategically in corners. There were even the mandatory portraits of ancestors marching down walls done in pale-ivory paper with delicate traces of flocked gold.

"What?" she asked. Defensively, he thought. Max glanced back at her.

"Where are the heads of state?"

"They're already seated."

Max threw back his head and laughed.

She realized she'd never heard him do that before. Deeply, and from his gut. He'd come close sometimes, but he'd never completely given himself over to it before. It pulled a smile from her when she'd thought five minutes ago that she would never smile again in this lifetime.

Dani closed the door behind him and lifted a mitted hand to rub at an itch on her nose.

"Bad move," he said, sobering a little. He reached out and touched the same spot.

Dani felt heat streak through her at his touch. She knew immediately what had happened. She'd left some of the beef burgundy there, the "perfectly simple but elegant" casserole her housekeeper had left for her to place in the oven at six o'clock. "I...uh, really get into my hobbies," she explained.

"To the point of wearing them?"

"When the situation seems to call for it."

He laughed again, this time a low, throaty chuckle. "What other hobbies are there? Besides sports, I mean." He didn't intend to give her the chance to try to convince him again that that was one of her passions.

"Gardening." The word was out before she knew she was going to say it.

"All those elaborate gardens out there are yours?"

She flushed. "Oh, no. The gardener does those."

"So where are yours?"

Her heart squeezed suddenly, once. "There aren't any."

He looked at her oddly.

"I stopped," she explained. "Why spend my time doing something that I pay someone else to do? Please, come in. Sit down."

"With the heads of state?"

"Um..."

She looked lost for a moment, Max thought. He waited.

"In the parlor," she said finally.

"You have one of those?"

A grin tugged at her mouth again. "Everything up to but not including a bowling alley. And Richard was going to add one of those just before he passed away."

Maxwell shook his head and said the wrong thing. "You weren't born to this any more than I was. How do you stand it?"

Her face closed down. "It's my life."

He wondered. She'd told him Danielle was who she was, too, but Roger had told him she'd identified herself as Dani when she'd called on Saturday.

He followed her into a nearby room. A drill sergeant couldn't have turned a neater corner, Max thought, cursing himself. She pivoted and headed for a door he'd previously missed—it was hidden between a large plant and a Chinese urn that, if it held the ashes of those ancestors on the walls, then it went back enough generations to include Adam and Eve.

Once again he took a moment to look around. This room was smaller, cozier, but maybe it just seemed that way in contrast to the immense center hallway. The furniture was heavy, upholstered in burgundy velvet. There was a fireplace. Wood had been laid in it, but it was cold.

"Oh, damn," she said suddenly.

"What?" He looked back at her.

Dani opened her mouth to tell him that she'd forgotten to start the fire. But that would have been a lie. She'd *tried* to light a fire in the hearth. She'd quickly discovered that it wasn't as easy to do as it looked. She'd gone back to the kitchen, thinking to return to it later. But moving premade recipes in and out of the oven had taken more time than she'd thought.

Admitting that would definitely not put her in a class with Morris Becker's wife.

"Sit," she said quickly instead. "Wait here. I'll be right back."

She hurried down the hall to the kitchen. She whipped the oven mitts off her hands as she went.

Dani was reasonably sure that she'd never cooked a meal before in her life. After her mother had died, she and her father had pretty much lived in motels and diners. When she had married Richard, he'd had a full staff. In between, there had been college and cafeterias and take-out pizza. Dani stood in the middle of the kitchen and looked around a little helplessly.

She could do this. She *could*. She had an M.B.A., for heaven's sake! Mrs. Dunley had taped little notes to each course, with directions about what to do with each one. Dani threw the oven mitts onto the stove and grabbed the little crab-filled mushroom caps from the counter. She touched a finger to one of them. She'd done them first according to the directions…many, many minutes ago.

They were cold now.

"Damn, damn, damn." Well, she thought, she knew microwaves. She'd heated up quite a few frozen dinners in school. She shoved the appetizer plate inside and slammed the door, hitting buttons.

The mushrooms came out steaming.

"Good," she muttered. "Perfect." She pivoted and headed back into the hallway, to the parlor.

Max was sitting in Richard's favorite overstuffed chair. It gave her a little jolt to see him there, then something warm curled in the pit of her stomach. She almost smiled…except Maxwell was examining his fingernails, clearly bored out of his mind.

Oh, no.

"Here you go," she said brightly. She moved to put the plate on the delicate table beside him. *Wine.* She needed the wine. That would be downstairs in the temperature-controlled wine cellar Richard had had built in. "Be right back."

She raced downstairs and grabbed what she wanted, along with two glasses. She stopped in the kitchen again to uncork the bottle. When she returned to the parlor, Maxwell was eyeing the plate of mushrooms.

She'd forgotten those cute little napkins that Mrs. Dunley had laid out along with the pretty forks and serving plates. "Finger food," she decided. She deposited the wine on a table near the cold fireplace, then she sat quickly in the chair opposite his. She grabbed a mushroom and popped it in her mouth.

And scalded her tongue.

Dani pressed her lips together and swallowed a squeal. She prayed that the stinging tears of pain in her eyes wouldn't show. She leaped to her feet and went to the other table, pouring the wine. She turned back to him.

"To your plovers." She raised both glasses, then she downed half of hers and felt the immediate relief to her tongue and the roof of her mouth. She breathed again.

"I'm sure they'll appreciate the sentiment," Max said, cocking his head a little to the side as he watched her. "So where are you going to put them? To the right or left of your hotel?" Calmly he lifted a mushroom and laid it on his own tongue.

Dani stared as he swallowed. Either he had a pain threshold that prisoners of war would kill for, or the damned things had cooled down. She reached for another one tentatively. Then she registered what he had said and her hand fell away.

"Something has happened," she said.

He had a clever way of smiling, she thought, that melted her soul. "What makes you say that?"

"To the right or left of my hotel? The senator's land is to the right of my original site."

"Your fund purchased that this afternoon. Senator Roberson saw the good sense in your suggestion and let you buy it."

"Ha." She'd been too busy worrying over this meal to realize it. And she'd given up control of that money, anyway, when she'd donated it. But *someone* should have called and told her, she thought. Someone like him. "Why didn't you call me and tell me?"

"I did. Your secretary said you left at three to make dinner."

She felt a blush try to creep up her neck. "It's going to be a hell of a meal."

He laughed again.

"So what you're telling me is that—in a matter of speaking—I own pretty much all of Gold Beach now," she said. "My two parcels, and my fund owns the other one."

"Hmm. It's all yours, except for the lot at the far end of Stan's."

"Who owns that?"

"I do."

Dani choked on her wine. "The coalition, you mean," she said when she could talk again.

Max stood to get the bottle. "No. Me personally." He topped off her glass.

"They must pay you well."

His chuckle filled the air between them again, low and rich. "I got a very good deal on the parcel."

"How much?"

He lifted a brow at her.

"It's a matter of public record," she reminded him.

"Point taken. Okay. I picked it up for a hundred bucks."

She nearly dropped her wine. *"What?"*

"There's more than one way to fight this battle. That is, besides hurling millions of dollars about."

"Who sold it to you for a hundred dollars?"

"Stan did. He owned two parcels. You really ought to speak to your research department about being more diligent."

She wasn't given to swearing, but a lot of vile words sprang to mind. "What are you going to do with it?"

"Find a way to force you out and turn the whole stretch of Gold Beach over into a preserve."

Dani opened her mouth to protest that—then she smelled the smoke.

"Something's burning," Max said.

"Be right back."

Dani vaulted out of her chair and tore down the hallway. *What could it be?* As near as she could remember, she had just turned the oven to low to keep the beef warm when he'd knocked on the door. *Nothing* could burn at warm—could it? She hit the swinging kitchen door with her shoulder and stumbled inside, looking around.

The oven mitts were on fire. She'd tossed them on top of the stove to take the mushrooms to the parlor! Had she left a burner on, too? *Yes!* To boil water for the noodles!

Dani raced to the counter. She hadn't boiled the water.

The pot was still sitting on the counter. She picked it up and heaved it. With a hiss and a belch of steam, the oven mitts became a charred, soggy mess on the range top.

Now what? She turned shakily and went back to the parlor.

Max had finished the mushrooms. That was good, she thought, because she really didn't think the rest of the meal was going to be all that filling. "Dinner is served," she said, clasping her hands together in front of her.

He looked at her, startled. "Was it repairable? Whatever went up in flames?"

"It was just some cotton and some stuffing."

"Ah, my favorite. Too bad."

She stared at him, then she laughed until her stomach hurt.

"Want to order Chinese?" he offered.

Dani pressed a hand to her tummy to steady the rolling nerves there. He was so kind, she thought. So unflappable. Confident even in the face of disaster. "Absolutely not," she answered. "I'm really very good at this."

"Okay. Lead the way."

She hurried down the hall to the dining room. *This* she had done well, though she suspected she'd obsessed over it. She'd debated between candles on the table—too romantic—and the colder light of the chandelier. She'd tormented herself over a tablecloth or place mats. The good china or the everyday stuff? She'd decided on the everyday stuff. Knowing Richard, it would be comparable to the rest of the world's good china.

She'd left the candles burning nicely on the sideboard and had turned the chandelier to low. She'd used the place mats. They'd seemed more business-dinnery, even if the corporate mogul had romance on her mind.

He'd pulled a chair out for her and was waiting for her to sit. "Um...no," she said, shaking her head. "I've got to get our dinner first."

"Need any help?"

"Of course not. I've got this absolutely under control."

He hesitated, then simply nodded. He was wise, too, she decided. He knew when to cease and desist.

Dani retreated to the kitchen. She pulled the beef burgundy from the oven—without noodles—and snagged the salad Mrs. Dunley had made from the refrigerator. She took them to the dining room and, on her second trip, she caught the French bread she'd sliced and put in the basket the housekeeper had left out for her. She grabbed butter—and that was as good as it was going to get.

He'd served up the beef, but he had waited for her. Dani dropped her napkin onto her lap as she slid into the chair beside him. "You're good at this," she murmured.

"At pretending my hostess knows how to cook?" He grinned.

"I can cook!"

He took a bite of the beef and looked surprised. "Actually, yes, you can. This is great." He spooned up more.

Dani's own bite went sour on her tongue. She swallowed quickly and thought about confessing that Mrs. Dunley had made it. But that would negate her whole plan of being so very domestic that Maxwell would just have to see her again.

"So, what's the verdict with your two parcels of

land?'' he asked, breaking her thoughts. ''Tell me, Dani, what do I have to do to wrestle them away from you?''

Wrestle? Dani took another bite and forgot to swallow. It brought images to mind, things she *knew* Danielle would never have considered. ''Ah...victor takes all?'' she ventured.

He wasn't going to touch that one, Max thought. He opened his mouth and answered, ''That's the way it generally works.''

''I have three parcels—in a manner of speaking—and you have one. I have more to lose.''

''I doubt that.''

It came quickly, too quickly, he thought, too deeply from his heart. His voice was fierce. Max pulled himself back from the brink. He rephrased his question. ''What can I do to convince you to see reason?''

Dani felt the air go out of her. There it was again, that quick little sidestep whenever she thought she might be reaching past his barriers. She forced herself to shrug. In truth, she hadn't given it a moment's thought. She'd been too worried about the details of this dinner. She opened her mouth and closed it again. She *had* ostensibly invited him over to try to change her mind.

''I'm going to build a resort there,'' she said finally. ''Unless you can think of a better reason why I shouldn't, something with a little more punch than good PR.''

''Not on your original site, you're not.''

''It's a temporary injunction. The clock's ticking.''

''We'll see. What about the other parcel?''

''Gardens.'' She had no idea where that had come from, but she opened her mouth and it fell out.

''The plovers' poor little wings are never going to hold out all the way to Mexico.''

Ouch. Dani straightened in her chair. "You really do think I'm heartless."

"The plovers won't stop on Gold Beach, Dani, not if there's any sign of habitation anywhere along that area of coast. Let the coalition buy you out. I'll raise the money. Build somewhere else."

"No." *It had to be that land.* Dani closed her eyes briefly and when she opened them again, his smile was gone.

"I don't understand you," he said finally. "Why are you so stuck on that site?"

"I'm not—" she began, then she broke off in horror. Belatedly the smoke alarm went off in the kitchen.

"Oh, *damn* it!" she cried. She threw her napkin on the table and launched from her chair.

In the kitchen she looked around wildly. It was still vaguely smoky, and she remembered Mrs. Dunley complaining that the handyman needed to check the batteries in the smoke alarms. Either he had and they were overjuiced, or he'd forgotten and they were malfunctioning. The alarm kept bleating.

At her wit's end, near tears, Dani stalked into the pantry. She found the fire extinguisher on the far wall. She grabbed it, wrestled with it a moment, and when it started hissing out foam she went back into the kitchen. She aimed it at the smoke alarm and let it rip. When the thing was covered in foam and still hiccuping, she sat at the kitchen table and lowered her head to the wood.

If the way to a man's heart was indeed through his stomach, then she was doomed.

Chapter Eight

Ice cream seemed safe enough. Nothing could go seriously wrong with ice cream.

Dani took it shakily back to the dining room, then she left hers untouched as she watched Maxwell clean his bowl down to the last drop. He seemed to enjoy it better than anything she'd presented so far—her premade, supermarket-purchased Rocky Road. It was a sad commentary on the outcome of her domestic efforts.

"Would you like a nightcap? Brandy? Sherry?" she asked when he pushed his bowl back.

"I should go."

Her heart stalled.

Go? Of the two hours he'd been here, she felt as though she'd had maybe ten minutes with him. She'd spent most of the time racing back and forth between the kitchen, the parlor, the dining room. No wonder Morris and Millie Becker had been together for thirty-six years. They probably never saw each other.

Dani cleared her throat. "It's early yet."

"And it's a work night."

"Mama puts you to bed by ten?"

She wasn't prepared for the change in his face. Something spasmed there, hard and sharp. What nerve had she touched?

He was going to go.

She wanted quiet time in the library, soft words, hidden smiles. Who gave a damn about resorts or birds any longer? She wanted to know why his face had changed in just that way at just that time. But the birds were all she had.

"We still have four parcels of land and not a place for a plover to rest," she murmured.

"That is all too unfortunately true."

"So what are we going to do about it?"

"I don't know, Dani. I've pretty much done all I can. I'd say it's up to you from here on in."

That didn't sound good. It sounded as though—new land or no new land—he was going to give up the fight. It sounded as though she would have her resort...and Maxwell Padgett would go from her life.

No.

She didn't know what came over her—frustration, desperation, maybe just a rush of need stronger and fiercer than she could tamp down. Dani pushed her chair back, then she stood, her hands fisted. She was definitely not thinking Danielle thoughts now. She knew that, and her heart galloped. But what could she do? What else could she possibly do?

She'd given him opportunity...and he'd politely slid away. She'd toyed, she'd teased...and he'd parried her, thrust for thrust, before disappearing.

The hell with that. Maybe, she thought, just maybe she shouldn't give him a choice any longer.

"What are you up to now?" Max's gaze lifted to her. The candlelight tangled in her hair, turning it to gleaming onyx. He wondered if that was why his legs felt suddenly too weak to lift him, to make him stand. Her eyes glittered. It was the chandelier light, he told himself.

Or pure feminine fire.

Snapping, crackling temper.

Fierce and humbling need.

She leaned across the table and curled her fists in the front of his sweater. And then, though he would have thought it was impossible, he found himself on his feet. And his mouth was fused on hers.

She'd kissed him first. He told himself that. She'd caught him by surprise. It swept away some of the guilt because he went on kissing her, anyway. Went on tasting the wine on her tongue and drawing her quick little gasp into his own lungs. He felt her go liquid in his arms, melt and give herself to him so simply, so sweetly…and entirely. His hands found her hair, cupping her head. And things happened inside him. Wanting her swerved into tenderness. Hunger reared and crashed and rolled.

Dani poured everything she had into the touch of his mouth on hers. She let loose with all the waves of heat inside her. She thought she felt his lips soften. But then his hands found her shoulders, and he set her away.

He was setting her away. How could he do that? Hadn't he felt what she had? *How?*

"Dani, I've got to go," he said hoarsely. Now, he thought, right now before he gathered her in his arms and carried her up those massive stairs to the bed he was sure to find on the second floor.

"This makes no sense," she whispered.

He almost stroked her hair, stopped himself. "It does."

"Then *tell* me. Tell me why."

It would have been easy, and maybe he owed it to her, Max thought. Maybe...but his conversation with Stan rolled around in his head again, echoing. What had he said? *There's nothing I can say to you that I can't say to her.*

When a man shared that way—shared those things—it was over.

"I had no business coming here," he said. "I'm sorry."

Sorry? Dani wondered if there were two worse words in the English language than that, after you had just kissed a man. She'd kissed precious few men in her life, but this had been different, and something told her that it was not something anyone should be sorry about.

Dani watched dazedly as he left the room. She wouldn't have thought she could walk, but she did. She followed him along the hall and caught up with him at the door. She cleared her throat. It hurt. Maybe mortification was a physical thing, she thought, something that turned everything in your body to stone. She lifted her arms to hug herself and they felt heavy.

"Now what?" she asked. She had to know, had to hear him say it. He was going to quit the fight.

He angled a glance her way. "I'm going to try to hold on to that injunction as long as humanly and legally possible. I figure it will take you a while to get all the permits on that other stretch, the new land. With any amount of luck, the plovers will have come and gone by the time you break ground. They don't stay long, six to eight weeks at most. They'll get one last nesting season in." He smiled, but it was a tight expression. Then he doffed an imaginary hat to her. "I'm beginning to accept that nothing is going to dissuade you. You're one very tough lady to do business with."

It should have been a compliment. Dani flinched. She didn't want to be a corporate maven. There were other needs, other aches, deep in her heart. She wanted to be a woman.

He'd kissed her and pushed her away.

They stepped out onto the porch between the massive ivory pillars. The breeze hit her. Dani shivered. When he left, when she went back inside into that big empty house, she knew it was going to be even colder.

"I'll put a hedgerow up," she blurted, remembering her original idea before this had gotten so complicated.

He looked startled as he took his keys from his pocket. "What good will that do?"

"I'll build on the new lot. Forget the golf course." She took a deep breath and hurried on. "I'll leave my original site vacant and that will give the birds three whole lots to themselves—including the one the fund bought and yours. I'll put a hedgerow up between them and my development and the birds will have privacy."

He was looking at her disbelievingly. "Dani, I've told you, that won't work."

"But *why?*" She felt on the verge of tears. She wanted him and she wanted her resort on Gold Beach. Why couldn't she have both?

Because he didn't want her. Maybe, she thought, she'd been misreading his signals all along.

"One change—one single change—and they'll keep on flying," he said.

Dani hesitated, then she nodded. They sounded like selfish little beasts to her.

He stepped down off the porch and glanced back at her. "Dani, go back inside. You're shivering."

"I want to see you off."

"You already have."

She wanted to give him every opportunity to kiss her again, to somehow fix everything that had just gone wrong between them. She wanted to understand why he hadn't wanted to keep kissing her...and more. She had been so sure he was attracted to her! It was in the way he had looked at her at the beach site when the news crews had been filming them. It was in the way he was aware enough of her to be nervous about it. Men who were aware, men whose eyes went smoky and hot, wanted to kiss...didn't they? She wasn't a fool, Dani thought. She couldn't be that wrong.

And for a moment, just a moment, he *had* kissed her back. Yet now he was leaning back against his Jeep door, his arms crossed over his chest, just watching her, making no move to reach out for her.

"I wouldn't have taken you for a Jeep kind of guy," she said. Anything to keep him talking, to keep him from leaving...once and for all. "I pictured you in... I don't know, maybe a Cadillac."

"Stan drives one of those. I like the beach, the mountains, and this takes me there."

"I guess I don't know you as well as I thought."

That earned a fleeting grin from him. "You never knew me. You just sized me up."

"That's not true!"

"Of course, it is. It's something someone like you does with the competition."

Someone like her? Oh, it hurt. "Obviously, you don't know me, either."

"I'd like to."

Her heart somersaulted. Her gaze flew fast to his own. Then she looked away because she didn't want him to see how nakedly she wished it could be true.

"I'd like to know why you're stuck on that particular stretch of beach beyond any sense of reason," he continued quietly. "I'd like to know what you do in this big house by yourself. I'd like to know how it happened that Richard Harrington and Michael Dempsey never tore the innocence out of you."

With each word he spoke, another small piece of her melted. Dani's eyes came back to him slowly, widening. He'd pushed off the Jeep and had taken a step closer to her. Need swept through her again, so big and deep she hadn't known she was capable of it. She swayed toward him, closing her eyes.

"But you won't tell me," he murmured. "Will you?"

Her eyes flew open again. How many kinds of fool could she be? And how many times in one night?

"Maybe I'm wrong, but I don't think you *want* to disenfranchise those birds. Your corporate antennae are just getting in the way of your heart."

He might as well have driven a knife into her chest. Dani stepped back quickly. "That's cruel."

"It's what I see. I just can't seem to get you to bend on this."

She froze. "Is that what this is all about? The *plovers?*" Of course, it was, she thought. Now she understood. He was trying to manipulate her into giving up, giving in. But—*damn him*—he was gentleman enough and arrogant enough not to take everything else she offered him in the process, to brush it aside.

All he wanted was to save his damned birds, to win another coup for the senator!

Dani took another step backward. One minute she'd

thought he was seeing into her soul. Then he tore that soul apart. "I'm going in. I'm cold." And the temperature in there, with Richard's ghost, would be warmer, after all.

He didn't say anything to hold her. Dani hurried for the steps and ran through the door, shutting it firmly behind her.

The hall was silent. But at least, she thought, it was a silence that knew and understood her. It was a silence that couldn't hurt her. She walked woodenly to the kitchen to begin cleaning up.

Roger Kimmelman stared at the closed door to his boss's office on Friday afternoon and frowned. This was a new wrinkle, he thought, one he wasn't quite sure what to do about. It had gone on for four days now—since Maxwell's Monday-night dinner with Dani Harrington— and it needed to be addressed. Besides, he knew something that might cheer the man up.

At slightly past three o'clock, he found the temerity to knock on Max's door.

"What?" his boss growled.

"I have an update on the plover situation."

"Then come in and give it to me."

Roger opened the door and stepped over the threshold. "Is everything all right, sir?"

Max's brow lowered. "Everything is fine. Why?"

"You seem…distressed."

"I haven't yet hung myself from the overhead lights, Roger. Relax."

"No, sir, of course not." He hesitated, then he asked, "Why, exactly, would you?"

Why? Max thought. Because the woman was a witch. And because he'd been harboring the sure sense all week that he'd hurt her deeply. But he had only spoken the truth…hadn't he? No matter what signals she seemed to throw off of a softer, gentler side, she wouldn't budge on the bird issue. There could be no reason for that other than the money she stood to make.

As for the other, he had done the right thing. He had not taken anything from her that he couldn't give back.

He had to put her out of his mind.

"What's the update?" he asked shortly.

"Ah." Roger cleared his throat. "I just got a phone call from one of our people in the field. The plovers are back."

Max sat straight in his chair. "They're at the site?"

"A couple of dozen of them have arrived so far. There should be hundreds by tomorrow."

"Yes." Max sat back again. "We've won, then. She can't break ground in the next six weeks before they finish nesting."

"Well, she could, but not if we manage to hold the injunction for a little while longer. And I learned that the zoning board won't meet on her new lot for another month." Roger cleared his throat. "Obviously, sir, something else is bothering you."

Max felt his jaw harden. It was an instinctive, knee-jerk response. He did not share easily. He knew better.

But this was tearing him up inside. Where was Stan when he needed him? Probably on some romantic get-away with Marcy, no doubt. Max hadn't been able to reach his friend all week.

Max came to his feet so hard and fast that his chair shot back, cracking against the wall behind him. "Let me tell you what she's doing." He heard his own voice and thought he was probably out of his mind. Roger was an *employee*. But the words spilled out of him, anyway, hot and tormented. "She wore a red lace bra and she let me see it!"

Roger's eyes popped. "Sir? When?"

"At the beach that day! In front of the cameras!"

"Ah, well, yes. You did seem distracted."

"Then she pretended she liked baseball and she didn't know a damned thing about it!"

"Um…was she bored?"

"Well…no," Max allowed. She definitely hadn't been bored. "But then she pretended she could cook!"

"Can she?" Roger asked.

"Well, yeah, the end result was great. But it was a rough and wild ride getting there."

"So maybe she *can* cook but she was just nervous. Either that, or she had her staff prepare the meal and she just served it herself."

Max felt as if he had been punched. He'd never thought of that. "*Why?* Why in the world would she do something like that? And why the holy hell would she grab me and kiss me when I did nothing—*nothing*— to prompt it?"

Roger's voice rose a notch. "She did that?"

"She did that," Max snapped.

"Well, it would seem that she's trying to hook you, sir."

Maxwell sat down again. Fast. "Hook me?"

"Red lace, baseball, home cooking and kissing only add up to one thing. Oh, and then there's the land."

"The land," Max repeated.

"The extra land. Why else would she have bought that second parcel except for the fact that you were about to walk away from this entire situation? It kept you actively involved. I believe she wants you around for a long haul."

"I haven't even given her the short haul yet!" Max exploded.

"*Yet* may be the operative word here, sir."

He couldn't breathe, Max realized. It was true. Stan was right. This was how it happened. All his air was stuck somewhere between his throat and his chest.

No one was going to hook him. *Ever.* Because he was a man no better than the rest of them, and he was damned if he was going to make promises he'd only break later. Because she was a woman better than most, and she deserved more than that.

"My advice to you may be to…ah, step back," Roger said. "Quickly. That is, if you don't want this."

"I tried that," Max growled.

"Roger? I'm waiting…and I hate to wait."

Max's eyes flew to the door. He saw a drop-dead gorgeous woman with a lot of blond hair in a very short dress. "Who are *you?*" Max demanded.

"She's with me," Roger said quickly.

"No, dear. I *was* with you before you saw fit to abandon me and come in here." She faced Max. "I'm Angelique Bonner. I work for Danielle Harrington. And I already know who *you* are."

Her eyes shot daggers. Yes, Max thought, he had hurt Dani Harrington.

"Well," he said dryly to Roger. "You've turned out to be quite the authority on women."

Roger actually blushed. "Am I through here, sir?"

"You're through."

Roger left—in a hurry. Max put a hand to his eyes, leaned back in his chair again, and groaned.

Dani was trying to "hook" him. He hadn't seen that at all. He'd just thought she was…quixotic. Maybe a little hyperaggressive in her interests.

Now he understood the baseball phenomenon. And of course her staff had cooked the meal, though she had certainly labored in getting it to the table. And the lace? Well, it had planted a hook. He couldn't deny that, since his first glimpse of it, it had kept haunting his mind.

But then there were all those things about her that spoke of lonely innocence. Where did they come in? They couldn't be by design…though they had haunted him, also.

She was trying to hook him.

It should have angered him. But on Dani Harrington, the whole business was endearing. Provocative. Flattering. Touching. And that was the most terrifying thing of all.

She made him want to believe. Because she did.

"I've gotten us a hearing on the twenty-ninth," said Morris Becker.

"What?" Dani looked up at her staff attorney. Her notes on the beach site were spread all over the conference room table. They were hashing the situation out…again. But her mind had wandered.

"To lift the injunction," Becker said at her blank look. "I've gotten us a hearing two days before groundbreaking. We could still be on target if we win."

"Oh. That's good."

Her staff and the board exchanged looks.

"Well, I've got that other lot," she said quickly, catching their reaction to her indifference. "I figure that if worse comes to worst, I'll just sign it over to the corporation and we can build there."

Someone cleared their throat. "That would require surveys, permitting…we'd be back to square one."

She felt her temper spark. That had been happening a

lot this week. "Do you think that has somehow escaped me? I've already moved ahead with all of those things, just to be on the safe side."

"There's always that property we own inland, in the peaks," another of the board members ventured. "It's suitable and we've already had that surveyed."

Dani shook her head. "No. I want Gold Beach."

As she spoke her mind wandered back to one simple, painful fact: Maxwell Padgett did not want her. He'd made that as clear as the moon on a star-filled night. As it turned out, he didn't even really *like* her. That had just been an act to soften her up and get her to do what he wanted her to do with the land. And when she'd resisted, he'd pushed her away.

He'd said terrible things about her character.

Therefore, there was only one thing left to her, Dani reasoned. She was going to move forward with the dream that had started all this.

"Max Padgett will fight us on the new Gold Beach plot, too," she snarled. "It's all a political game for him." *She* had been a political game. And it still hurt down to her bones. "But when it comes to games, I'm better. We'll have Gold Beach. I promise you."

She left the conference room and went back to her office. There she found an unprecedented note stuck to her blotter…from Angelique. "Took off early," it said. "I have vacation time coming. See you Monday. PS— the birds have come back to Gold Beach."

What the hell? Dani sat at her desk and covered her face with her hands. The world was going to hell in a handbasket.

Chapter Nine

She was out of her mind, Dani thought six hours later. This was the last place in the world she should want to be. But she stopped her BMW in front of her original Gold Beach site, anyway, then she sat there, shivering and staring.

It was late, after ten o'clock. She'd gone home and had roamed the house with an ache in her bones. And all she kept thinking was, *those birds are back.*

For what it was worth, she'd realized that she had to see them.

She wondered if her father had ever encountered them here. What would Richard have done if he had known about them? She thought she knew the answer to that. Black ink had always been the bottom line for Richard. It was, after all, where she had truly learned the art.

Dani turned the heat to high, then she got out of the car, anyway. It was only a week shy of May, but the air was frigid. An emphatic wind swept off the sea, biting through her suit jacket, ruffling her hair. She hadn't bothered to change when she'd gone home. Too much had been gnawing at her heart, too much had been in her head. She'd sipped a glass of sherry and had paced that big empty house.

Now she kicked off her high heels and left them by the car. She began to pick her way through the dunes to the surf. Where were they? She had come to see birds, and they were nowhere to be found.

"This is only the first handful of them. These are the leaders of the pack. Over the next few hours the rest of them will flock in."

Maxwell.

Dani jolted and looked around to see him step out of the dunes. The first warmth in days seemed to fill her chest...and that angered her. What right did he have to leave her cold without him?

"What are you doing here?" she demanded.

"Probably the same thing you are."

She shook her head and caught her hair back from blowing into her eyes. She forced herself to remember the way he had tried to manipulate her to make her change her mind about her lot. "I doubt that," she muttered. *She* wanted to stone the critters.

It wasn't true, but he'd made it clear that that was what he expected from her.

He held a hand out to her. "Come on. I'll show you the plovers."

"No."

"Please?"

Dani closed her eyes. In spite of everything, she yearned to grasp on to him and to keep holding on. But he wasn't what he seemed. The he stepped closer to her and his hand slid from her elbow to her wrist, then his fingers twined with hers. And she had no defenses against that.

"Don't be stubborn," he muttered.

"I'm not stubborn."

"You're the most hardheaded woman I've every met."

"I am not."

"Then come see the birds."

She tugged against him once, twice. But then, why had she come here except to see them? And besides, indifference to him was really the best approach.

Dani finally stopped resisting. "How did you get here?" It occurred to her to ask as they climbed through the rest of the dunes. If she had seen his vehicle, she wouldn't have stopped. Of course she wouldn't have.

"I left the Jeep farther down the dunes."

"Roaming the beaches in your four-wheel-drive again?"

"I drive the shore whenever I can. I live on the beach. I have a town house a few miles up the coast."

"Ha. No displacing wildlife there."

"Seagulls aren't endangered."

She was losing every argument she started.

"There." He pointed when they had left the dunes behind. "I parked about a quarter of a mile down."

"So as not to give any little avians a heart attack?" Her hand felt too good in his. *Damn him.* "Don't worry about it. There are no constituents here to notice." Her words fell into a long silence.

"Is that what you think of me?" he asked finally.

"I don't know what to think."

"That makes two of us." Then he pulled her to a quick stop. "Shhh. We'll scare them."

"Footsteps will scare them?" But Dani paused and looked around.

Then she saw them. There really weren't many—he was right about that. They gathered at the scalloped edge of the waterline, tiny frantic things on spindly legs. Darting here, darting there. They were cute, she thought. Intent.

Then three or four little heads popped suddenly in their direction. Wings ruffled. They skittered into the surging edge of the sea. As though some silent voice had called to all of them, the remaining dozen or so streamed after them.

Maxwell hadn't been lying. They seemed scared to death.

"Each one of them could fit in my hand," Maxwell said quietly. "If something came along that was big enough that you could sit in its hand, wouldn't you be afraid? Think what the roar of a bulldozer would do to them."

"I hate you."

Her voice was so low, so intense, it robbed his breath. She meant it, he realized, at least in that moment. She jerked free of him, and something drove hard and cold into his chest.

He'd hurt her again. But how? By making the birds real, by disrupting her corporate single-minded aim? Damn it, *he* hadn't brought her here tonight. She'd come on her own.

She'd come on her own.

Max watched her run for the shoreline. For the first time he realized she was barefoot again. He'd watched the green BMW creep up to the site. Her headlights had caught his attention as he'd sat on the beach. He'd watched her get out, drawn by something he couldn't see, as she came through the dunes. But he hadn't noticed her kicking her shoes off.

There was a part of her who was happiest with sand between her toes, he realized. *That* had been the woman in red lace who'd confronted him on television. And she had been barefoot on Monday when she'd made him dinner—or whatever she had done with that meal—as well.

Max went after her. But before he reached her, she did something astounding. She reached the shoreline…and she sat down. Suit and all. In the wet sand. A wave came up and just tickled the hemline of what could only be a dry-cleaned skirt.

He stopped short, just behind her. "Dani, what is it?"

"I can't care about those birds. I *can't.*"

"I'm sorry."

"I'm not killing them. I just want them to lay eggs elsewhere. I even offered to share the land!"

He approached again. He sat beside her—in the lick of the waves—and felt the ice-cold water creep into the legs of his jeans. "I didn't mean to hurt you."

"Well, there's an ego for you," she muttered. "*You* have nothing to do with this. You just pointed the problem out to me."

"Tell me then. Tell me what's wrong."

"No. You already think I'm terrible. Let's leave it at that."

That rocked something inside of him. Had it sounded that way to her? "No," he said. "I don't."

"You think I'm stubborn and coldhearted because I have to build my resort here."

"Why does it have to be Gold Beach?" he asked again.

"Because it's a spectacular site." She lifted her head. Her chin came up and she stared out at the moonlit sea.

There had to be more to it than that, he thought.

"And because I'm winning."

Max frowned. "Our fight? Yes, I'd say you've won."

Things ached inside her again. Dani drew her knees closer. She rested her chin on them. Somehow, she thought, amazingly, the plovers were coming back. Oh, they were giving them a wide berth. Twenty feet at least, she thought, on each side. But they were starting to stream around their quiet, sitting forms and skitter their way toward the dunes again.

"They're the males," Maxwell said. "They'll sort of pummel the nesting site and get it ready before the females come along to mate tomorrow. The ladies will probably be here by morning."

"How quintessential." But her voice cracked.

"Hey, it's worked since Adam and Eve, since Tarzan and Jane."

"As far as I'm concerned, Eve blew it with that damned apple."

He laughed. He hadn't meant to, but he laughed.

"All the same," she continued, "I guess it's the standard meant to be followed. The males build the homes and protect, the females mate and feed their young."

"Maybe it's just that the brighter a species gets, the more ways it can find to tear up a perfectly simple and workable status quo."

Something in his voice alerted her. It was that same kind of spasm that had crossed his face when she'd mentioned his mother. She waited for him to say something more, but he only turned the conversation back to her.

Sidestepping again, she thought. It was emotional as well as physical. Why hadn't she noticed that before?

"What about you?" he asked. "Why haven't you had children? You were married for several years."

Something inside her tried to crack. But she'd been asked before, and she had the answer down pat. "I've nurtured the corporation instead. That's what Richard asked of me." She tried to make her voice hard again— he expected it of her. "I've made Harrington Enterprises a great deal of money. My instincts are good."

"I don't doubt it."

No, she thought, he wouldn't doubt *that* part of her. "It's what I've got."

"The appreciation of a few board members?"

"I'm doing my job. If I don't do my job, they could yank it all away from me." And then, Dani thought, she would have nothing.

"They can't oust you."

"Of course they can. This is business."

"Your husband gave you Harrington Enterprises."

"My husband gave me thirty-nine shares of Harrington Enterprises. And I bought Angelique's ten. You weren't a business major, were you?"

"No. Marine biology with a minor in economics."

"Well, there you have it." She paused. "I think Richard set it up like this on purpose. To keep me on my toes so I can never neglect his baby. No one else holds more than five shares, but if they all stockpile their votes, yes, they could still get me out."

"So what? You've probably got more money than you can spend in this lifetime."

"They're my family."

Max felt something clench in his chest.

She waved a hand negligently. "You can't be expected to understand."

"I do."

"If no one else, you have Stan."

"He's as close as a brother, but he's not related to me."

"Does blood matter? He's *alive*."

And then Max thought he understood.

She turned on her hip to face him fiercely. "This resort is going to make a fortune. Right here. Facing the sea. And I'll have that board in the palm of my hand."

"There are plenty of other miles of sea." He'd said that before.

"But my father didn't bring me to those miles when I was a child."

Ah, Max thought. Everything inside him went still.

"He was never around much to begin with—maybe on Sundays. But then my mother died, and he was *never* there. So this was what I had of him...occasionally."

"But he took you with him on the road."

She laughed and he thought the sound might have hurt her throat. "Yes. I thought it was going to be wonderful, but it was just a new kind of isolation—motel rooms instead of anything familiar. I had tutors on the road, which turned out to be an excellent education and put me ahead of the rest of my peers. But I was always stuck in this motel or that one, studying, waiting for my father while he did what he had to do. I rarely saw him after my mother died. It was guilt. He'd left her to die on her own. He could never face the house again. I was with her that day. He couldn't face me."

"Dani..."

"Don't touch me," she said quickly. She felt him reach for her. She knew that if she found her way into his arms right now, she would never leave again.

And he didn't want that.

"Once in a while," she continued, "on Sundays when

we came home, we visited here. He was going to build here, you know.''

Max felt surprise filter through him. ''On Gold Beach?''

''He always promised me that someday he would retire and we would live here together. In a new home, one my mother didn't haunt. Of course, he never retired. He couldn't. He was running from himself. It was why he drove himself so hard.''

She couldn't have understood his heartache when she was twelve, he thought, not when Michael Dempsey was running from her. Max understood better than she knew.

''He had a heart attack when I was eighteen,'' Dani finished quietly. ''He really had put aside a lot of money for the house he wasn't ever going to build, and I used it to go to Stanford. It was all I knew.''

''School.'' He knew that she didn't want pity. But when he looked at her profile in the moonlight, spectacular and clean, that inky hair curling behind her ears, something cracked inside him for her. He got it now. He understood. She was going to erect a huge, glamorous monument to the few special times she had shared with a man who'd barely taken the time to know her. In the process she would solidify her position among a group of strangers so that they would never try to close her out.

With this land, this resort, she finally had control of her own life.

''If it's not political,'' she asked suddenly, changing the subject, ''then why won't you let me divert a few birds?''

''Because you don't really want to.''

''I want to very, very much.''

''In your heart you'll bleed for every feathered wing.''

"The way you expect me to believe you will?"

"Let *me* tell *you* something, Dani Dempsey Harrington." He was crazy, he knew he was crazy. Yet he traced a finger down her jaw anyway. And he felt her shudder beneath his touch. His voice went hoarse. And he let her in. "I've spent my entire adult life caring for anything—anyone—who doesn't have anyone else to care for them. Because I can. I told you Stan and I aren't related. We hooked up together in the system—you know, the one for kids who've been turned over to the state for one reason or another. Stan had run away and wouldn't tell anyone who his parents were, and the social workers couldn't find out. My mother died when I was three and no one ever knew who my father was. So we were both plopped down into foster homes. We crossed paths once in a while—they had these big public events where they paraded us out, hoping someone would adopt us—and we shared a home when we were sixteen. That was a bad one. We ran away together. Stan dogged me into finishing school. He made sure we got scholarships, that we went to college. We stuck together, rooming together, until adulthood pulled us in separate directions."

Dani stared at him. She hadn't known.

"Stan's stubborn, arrogant, outrageous sometimes, but I'd be dead without him. So even if I didn't have this urge to make sure nothing I come in contact with gets abandoned like I did, I'd *still* owe this to him."

"But you backed off," she whispered. "You backed off from our fight."

"I've done all I can do. You've beaten me."

She felt tears bite at her vision. "I need this land."

"No, Dani. You just need to be needed."

She came undone then. Because he was right. And because he wasn't the one who needed her.

She started to get up, trying to get away from him. One hand reached out and caught her about the waist. She tumbled back to his chest, and she felt his mouth at the back of her neck. Hot, wet, trailing kisses. Everything she'd wanted. And yes, everything she needed.

Dani rolled back toward him. And suddenly, his mouth was on hers again.

They cleaved together and her heart beat against his. His lips clung to hers. And there was so much more than passion in his kiss.

There was acceptance.

Chapter Ten

He didn't put her away from him this time, but he stopped all the same. His mouth slid to her neck, then he rested his forehead against hers. Dani found enough shaky breath to speak.

"If you're going to tell me you're sorry again, keep in mind that there's a whole ocean right here where I could dispose of your body."

Maybe he tried to laugh. She wasn't sure.

A lone plover stood watching them from ten feet away. She could see it over Max's shoulder. Every once in a while it made a little chattering sound and fluffed its wings as though it had a point to make.

Dani's nerves still thrummed, but she discovered in that moment that there were worse things than being pushed away. There was trying to hold on to someone who would rather go. She cared more for his obvious turmoil than her own need to stay in his arms. She eased free of his embrace, releasing him. A pang hit her heart when she realized how relieved he looked.

He stood to look out at the sea...and to put some space between them. *What the hell had he done?* He'd done exactly what he had been on the tender verge of doing for weeks now, and this time he couldn't plead innocence, could not say she'd started it. He hadn't even ended it.

He'd done the thing he'd been sane enough to fight...until she'd gone soft and shaky and needy right in front of his eyes, until they'd shared dreams and hurts and secrets.

He opened his mouth and the truth left him, unvarnished. "Dani, I'm not your kind."

She went still. She was sure she would shatter if she moved. "Do you really think that little of me?"

He brought his gaze back to her, startled. "I think that much of you. You deserve a man who's going to be with you for a while."

How could every word he said hurt worse than the last? Dani was spinning. The stars whirled above her head and she couldn't focus. "And wouldn't you be?"

"I save everything I can, and I refuse to destroy those things I can't."

"You think you'd *destroy* me?"

He smiled sadly. "I'm not even sure a man exists who wouldn't."

"I don't understand."

He pushed his hands into his jeans pockets. He didn't look at her. "Dani, I was in the system for thirteen years. I didn't have to be. There were relatives—okay, distant ones—on my mother's side who could have taken me in. None of them wanted to be saddled with a toddler, or worse, a prepubescent boy. So the state kept feeding me, but the roofs over my head kept changing because

I was, after all, just there for the families to collect an extra buck or two along the way.''

''That can't be true.'' She was appalled that that was the only reason people would take in unwanted children. Surely there was someone more altruistic out there. But Max shook his head.

''It was true more often than not. My point is, if I didn't stay invisible, I ended up out, moved on to the next home.'' He finally looked back at her. ''It's amazing what you can observe when you're trying to stay quiet enough to fade into the wallpaper. Love is nothing more than attraction, Dani. It's a flash in the pan and it burns out. I won't pretend to love anyone—not in the way the world defines the word. I want you. I've wanted you from the first—too much. The hotter the fire, the faster it burns. I won't take what you think you want to give only to walk away from you before you're ready to let me go.''

It was insulting—she *knew* she should be insulted, but she only hurt for him.

He started toward the sea, then he turned back. The moonlight turned his eyes to silver. ''I never knew my father, Dani, but I spent enough time in those foster homes to know men don't hang around. I've watched a lot of other men promise, and they didn't stay, either. And from what you've told me, you've been left alone enough. I'm sorry. I never should have engaged you in this fight.''

Her heart ached inside her chest. He was saying that the emptiness that had filled her whole life was inevitable. That it would never change. And she found that simply too tragic and overwhelming to bear. ''Don't go,'' she whispered.

He didn't seem to hear her. ''I'm not sure the plovers

need me as much as you need what this place means to you," he continued. "Concrete and glass will at least stay put, and I can't give you that. So do what you want with your land. I won't stop you. I'll lift the injunction on Monday morning."

No! Everything inside her coiled up in protest. She'd won...but she hadn't gotten what she needed.

Max made his way up the beach without another word. Behind her, Dani heard the steady ruffle of wings. It was the loneliest sound she had ever heard.

"Well, he's a *man*," Angelique proclaimed a little disgustedly. She'd come running at Dani's call, no doubt canceling plans to be there. It was Saturday night. Twenty-four hours had passed since Maxwell had left her on the beach. Thirty-six hours remained until he might actually lift the injunction as he'd promised.

Angelique sipped wine in Dani's parlor. Dani's stomach rolled, and she couldn't even nurse her papaya juice.

"And your point would be what?" she asked quietly. She still felt numb.

"That there are more where he came from."

"No." The word was hard and flat and it took even Dani by surprise. "I want *him*."

In the same moment, she heard his voice inside her head. *I'm not your kind.* That, she thought, was purely hogwash. He'd sailed through that abomination of a dinner with charm and kindness and not more than one—okay, maybe two—batted eyes. He was intelligent and gentle enough to honestly care about *birds*. She knew now that it wasn't just politics. It was because they were weak and helpless...and because they eventually flew away. She ached for the boy inside who thought that everything—everyone—eventually would.

She refused to believe he was right. If she accepted that everyone ended up alone sooner or later, then nothing else in life would ever be enough. Dani knew suddenly that the single thing that had taken her through life since her mother had died was hope…that her father would finally see her again, that Richard would finally look past the walls of the corporation and find her there.

That a man worth wanting would want her. And Max Padgett was that man.

He was clever and genuine and sometimes the emotions that went through him were so intense she could actually feel them in her own heart. Not her kind? They both knew the loneliness of being truly alone. And they both knew how precious a hand in the dark could be.

Dani put her glass down on the parlor table and crossed her arms over her chest. "I need a plan."

Angelique looked over at her, alarmed. "I've already told you that's what you *don't* need."

"No offense, but your advice has gotten me nowhere so far."

"It got you kissed a couple of times. And well, from the sounds of it. Be grateful for it and move on."

Dani's heart rolled over and her skin heated. There *was* that. "But I want more."

Angelique shrugged. "Have it your way. But don't say I didn't warn you."

"About what?"

"About whatever your plan nets you."

"You're going to *what?*" Stan hit the cue ball so hard it bounced clear off the green felt. It hit the floor and rolled into a far corner of his rec room.

"Lift the injunction," Max repeated, bending to retrieve the ball. "You lost. My game."

"You can't do that."

"Sure I can. The cue ball left the table. You forfeit."

"I'm not talking about the game and you know it."

"She needs that beach, Stan."

"I need those votes!"

Max looked at him with an expression that would have frightened someone who didn't know him so well.

"All right, all right." Stan held up a hand. "Let's slow down and talk this out."

"There's nothing to talk about. I'm not going to hurt her."

"You're sinking, friend. And you're bailing. On me."

Everything inside Max stiffened, hardened, until it hurt. He owed Stan a lot, but he was thinking of a little girl whose father had spent scant hours with her...but he had done it on that beach. He *could* give her something that would last, something she'd never find in a man's arms.

Suddenly, another thought hit him. Would it be enough? Or would she carry that sweet, earnest innocence, that bright and sparkling mind, to someone else, still looking for the one thing Max knew didn't exist? The idea of another man taking her in his arms made Max's stomach clench. He yanked his mind back from the image, but it resisted.

Dani deserved what her father hadn't given her and what Richard Harrington had apparently not thought important. But the thought of her rolling in the sand with anyone else stunned Max and left him numb.

"You're throwing me over for a woman?" Stan asked incredulously.

"What?" Max asked blankly.

"One you don't even intend to see again?" Stan continued. "What kind of sense does that make?"

Max got a grip on himself again. "All the sense in the world." He set his pool cue back in the rack. On that note, he was going home.

She'd gone about it all wrong, Dani realized on Monday morning. She'd asked Michael Axler what had first attracted him to Denise. She'd asked Morris Becker why he'd wanted to see more of Millie. But she hadn't asked any of them why they'd fallen in love.

She'd been bouncing a pencil on her desktop. Suddenly her thoughts froze and the pencil fell from her nerveless fingers. *Love?*

Was that what she wanted?

Everything inside her shook and shimmied. She wanted to spend more time with Maxwell because he made everything come alive inside her. And yes, she wanted to *be* loved again—someday, by someone, all the way. But did that mean she loved *him?*

Panic skittered inside her. She knew far too well what it was to love and be forced to let go. And he'd already warned her that he was bound to go.

It was hope, she thought again. She couldn't let go of it. It was just a matter of possibilities. Without them, life was nothing. And if her heart was crushed as she went in pursuit of them, then it got crushed.

Love?

That wild, edgy, needy feeling he brought to her was just a…a byproduct of their contest over her land. It was competition, and hormones and lust had a little to do with it, as well. The feeling had somehow gotten all tied up with her plot to wrest her resort free and clear of his clutches by appealing to his senses, and now, when she thought of that land, she did not think of a thirty-million dollar resort or sitting in her father's lap. She saw stars and plovers and Maxwell.

Dani rose from her chair and pressed her fingers to her temples, then she wandered dazedly into the hallway. Angelique was on the telephone, wearing a catlike grin. What was *that* all about? The question moved in and out of Dani's head then was gone.

"I need a meeting," she said.

Angelique hung up the telephone. "What kind of meeting?"

"I need every male in a chief management position." Then she thought about it. "Make that all department heads, male or female." It was a given that most women knew a lot more about this than she did. She looked at her watch. It was just past eleven. "Get everyone to the conference room by eleven-thirty."

She turned and went back into her office. What else was left? she wondered, sitting at her desk again. It was time to pull out all the stops...one last time. She'd been in this kind of situation before, albeit in a professional capacity. But she'd come up against situations where the only possible reaction was to do or die. How, really, was this so different? She wanted something. She'd make one last colossal pitch to get it.

She wanted Max, for as long as he would stay. And if she failed, then she would walk away.

It was the only sane thing to do, she decided. She'd always been a firm believer in being able to look herself in the mirror. In every situation of her life she'd needed to know, in her heart, that she had done all she was capable of doing. When that was the case, it had always helped her to accept it when and if she failed.

She stood again. Her legs didn't feel quite as rock-solid as they should, given her newfound conviction. She smoothed a hand over her deep-lilac skirt—Angelique's suggestion—and the nifty, short, matching jacket. She'd buttoned it all the way up because she wore only a camisole underneath. The tiniest peak of ivory lace showed at her lapels. These days she dressed for a hypothetical occasion…just in case Maxwell did something else outrageous and she found herself in a position to face him down again, one more time.

Unfortunately, there had been nothing but fresh silence from him since Friday.

It was eleven-thirty. Dani left her office and strode down the hall toward the conference room.

They were all there, all her department heads and her entire legal team. Dani stepped into the room and suddenly came to her senses. *What was she doing?* These people would think she was out of her mind! She'd lose everything. She'd be bounced out of Harrington Enterprises on her rear!

So what?

The sneaky thought rocked her, but what Maxwell had said was true. Without the job, she would hardly starve. And this was more important.

Besides, she thought, if these people decided that she was brilliant, she'd be secure for a long, long time. She decided it was all in the way she pitched this.

Dani cleared her throat. The idea bloomed, blossomed, spread. She put on her best CEO stance, her hands clasped loosely at her waist. She smiled calmly out at the faces gathered around the table. And she cloaked what she really wanted—tips on how to snare Maxwell—in terms of nailing that Gold Beach land once and for all.

"There's been a development with the resort site," she said. "However, I achieved it by somewhat…

unorthodox means." Looks were exchanged, but she caught one or two nods...people who'd always expressed faith in her from the start. Encouraged, she pushed on. "I've developed a friendship with Maxwell Padgett through all this. And I believe—because of it—that he might lift the coalition's injunction against our original site."

Morris Becker was the first to speak. "When?"

"My guess would be within the next forty-eight hours." That was safe, she thought. He'd told her today.

People were smiling, nodding.

"But now I need your help," Dani continued. "I want to go in for the kill to ensure that this happens. I'd like your feedback, your input. What's the best way to butter him up until I get what I want?"

Someone chuckled nervously.

"You want him eating out of your hand?" asked the head of her human relations department, a bright and attractive young man in his late twenties.

"Exactly." Dani nodded. "I want you to go back to your desks and write me a list of five things I might do to ease up the last of any resistance he may have against me. Feel free to be honest, because I want everything by computer printout—no handwriting. And, of course, don't put your names on the lists. You've got complete anonymity to suggest...well, anything at all that comes to mind. I'm going to have Angelique place a box here on this table when we're through. Just drop your list in and I'll take them under advisement at the end of the day."

Someone actually laughed. Dani smiled. "I know it's an unusual approach, but if I can pull this off, this resort will be the most spectacular we've done yet. I'll remember that you were all a part of this. If the resort makes us the money I foresee, I'll guarantee you all raises."

More laughter. *Very* good, Dani thought. She stepped back from the table. "Have at it." Then she quickly left the room.

She drudged her way through the rest of the day, tidying up loose ends, unable to concentrate. At three o'clock, she called the court. The injunction still had not been lifted. Her stomach was in knots.

On one level, she thought, that was good. It was very good. It meant that Maxwell still had not washed his hands of her and the situation. He still had not shut the door. On another level it was bad. Because if the two of them just kept trundling along as they had been, this could drag on for weeks yet and there would be no resolution. And she needed resolution. She needed to know once and for all if he was going to stay for a while...or if he was going to go.

At a quarter to five, Angelique knocked on her door. She had a box in her hands and it was stuffed full of paper. "I thought you might want to start going through this. I put a new one on the table for any late entries." Angelique put the box on her desk. "Would you like help with it?"

Dani looked up into her eyes and she saw there that Angelique knew exactly what she was up to, and it had nothing to do with the land. "What do you think about this?" she asked tentatively.

"I think it's a smashing approach. But I also have an inside track and I believe that Max Padgett is gone on you. He's just going to need some nudging along."

Dani's jaw fell. "*Gone* on me?" Then her brain cleared, and she suddenly remembered Angelique's recent furtive telephone conversations and that unprecedented day-off-without-warning. "*What* inside track?" she demanded.

"I've been seeing Max's aide."

Dani bolted straight upright in her chair. "The one with the blond hair and the razor-sharp trousers?"

"Yes."

Dani stared at her. "Since when did that become your style? I thought you were more into the bad-boy types."

Angelique grinned. "There's something refreshing and intriguing about integrity."

Dani thought of Max again and nodded bemusedly. She couldn't deny that.

Then she laughed. She laughed hard enough that tears came to her eyes. Maybe love made the world go around after all.

"Okay, sit down and let's find out what the rest of Harrington Enterprises thinks I should do about this."

Chapter Eleven

By the time they had emptied the second box, Dani's voice was a little hoarse from reading off the suggestions and she had a headache. She plucked out the last piece of paper. "One—wine and dine him."

"Check," Angelique said. She was working on a master list.

"Two—use feminine wiles."

Angelique rubbed her nose thoughtfully. "Would you say that falls into the same category of 'wow him with great sex' and 'seduce him'?" Then she nodded. "Yes, I would say so."

Dani felt her skin heat a little. It discomfitted her a little that her employees had homed in so directly on the heart of the matter. "Number three says to appease him, to set that new land I bought aside for a plover sanctuary." *And what fun would that be?* Besides, she thought, according to Maxwell that wouldn't work, anyway.

"What's four?" Angelique asked.

"Make a sizable campaign contribution to Senator

Roberson. And five says to marry him—Maxwell, not
the senator. Apparently, California's laws would forbid
him from holding the injunction against himself, and if
I married him those lots would be community property.''
Dani sat back. "Okay, give me the rundown. Now that
all the votes are in, what's the top suggestion?"

Angelique looked at her list. "The wow-him-with-
great-sex-slash-seduce-him-slash-use-feminine-wiles
idea.''

Dani had just taken a mouthful of lukewarm coffee
and it nearly came up her nasal passages. "Are you serious?"

"It appeared in one form or another on everybody's
lists. With good cause, I might add.''

"Did you put a list in here?" Dani demanded.

"Yup."

"What did yours say?"

"Stop planning and talking about it and get down to
business.''

"What else?"

"That was all.''

Dani digested that. "What was the first runner-up on
the master list?"

"The wining-and-dining him category. Would you
like my opinion?''

Dani nodded.

"Combine the two. Wine and dine him, then at the
end of the night, jump his bones. He won't offer you a
bit of resistance.''

Dani came to her feet. "I can't do that!" But why,
she wondered? Why couldn't she?

Angelique stood, as well. "Are we done with all
this?''

"We're done. But let me keep that master list." She

grabbed the page from her secretary's hand. Just in case she got cold feet and needed to fall lower down on the list and regroup.

Pull out all the stops. Her own thoughts of earlier in the day jangled around in her head. She poured herself another cup of coffee while Angelique collected the boxes and the papers and left her office.

Do it. She didn't dare. What she knew about seducing a man would fit on her thumbnail.

Do it. He'd slide away from her again like he had both times before, and having it happen *three* times in a row would be devastating.

Do it. She'd always been a traditional sort of person. The man should be the one to make a move like this, she thought. Then again, left to his own devices, *this* man probably wouldn't.

She decided to plunge in with both feet.

She went to the telephone and called the coalition. The phone rang and rang until Dani glanced at her watch. It was a quarter to six. He was probably gone for the day. Clearly, his staff was. She was about to hang up when there was a click and she heard his voice.

"Coalition for Wildlife, Fields and Streams."

Dani took a breath, swallowed air...and got down to business. "There's still an injunction against my land."

"Well, hello to you, too."

She thought she heard him sigh. It was a soft sound that touched her skin across the telephone line. Then he said her name. "Dani." Just her name, nothing more, and things inside her trembled.

She collected herself. "We could keep fighting," she suggested. "I was never entirely adverse to that."

"Unfortunately, your fight really is with Stan now and

not with me. He moved in court today to block me from unblocking you.''

Dani's brows climbed her forehead. It wasn't something she'd considered. ''This is getting complicated. I thought he was your best friend.''

''He is.''

''He's angry with you.''

''He'll get over it.'' But there was a tension in his tone now that Dani hadn't heard before.

''You're hurt,'' she murmured.

''Of course I'm not. It's business.''

''But he's putting it between you.'' And her entire heart hurt for him. *Someone else had taken a step back from him and put himself first.*

''Stan promised his constituents that nothing would ever happen to that land, to the birds there. Part of the reason he was elected was because of his close association with my coalition. Stan doesn't want to settle for one term.''

''What do *you* want? You gave in to me pretty easily on this.''

''I gave in suddenly, not easily.''

''Why?'' she persisted.

''I couldn't take any more of your stuffed mushrooms.''

''I thought you liked the mushrooms!''

''I couldn't taste them. They were too hot.'' His voice dropped a notch in that way it had. ''I enjoyed kissing you a lot more.''

Something unseen slammed her in the chest. She wasn't ready for that. ''You said you were sorry.''

''I am. And it won't happen again. But now that we've reached the end of the road, I want you to know that it's a memory I'll keep. I liked it, Dani. It's right up there with the year Santa Claus brought me a motor scooter.''

She laughed but the sound was tangled with hurt. "I'm surprised Santa was that generous within the state system.''

"He wasn't. That was what made it so special.''

That quelled her and made her yearn all over again.

"That year I was with a good family,'' he added.

"What happened? Why didn't you stay with them?'' She realized she was curled up in her chair now, her shoes off and her feet tucked under her. She cradled the phone against one shoulder.

His voice always had that effect on her.

"Their son didn't like me,'' Max said.

"What did you do to him?''

His laughter filled the line. "What makes you think I did anything?''

Because she knew the way he fought. "You broadsided me with hundreds of placard-carrying protesters. You snatched up that other parcel of land for a hundred bucks. And you sneaked an injunction in on me.''

"True.'' He paused. "I like to win.''

"Then why are you quitting now?'' Don't quit, she thought. Please don't quit on me.

"This time I can't afford to lose.''

Her head hurt. "Your coalition can't have won every battle they've started.''

"No, we haven't. And I can live with that. But I'm not going to break your heart.''

There it was again…and her heart was already squeezing.

He was quiet for a moment. "I'm just your average guy,'' he said finally. "Stan's the one with the aspirations. I just want to get through life without hurting anyone too much, maybe saving a creature or two along the way. One of these years I'll turn the coalition over to Roger. Maybe I'll buy some land and rescue abused pets. Maybe I'll run for political office myself, or start a decent orphanage for throwaway kids. I don't know. But whatever it is, I'll do it for a while and move on. Because that's the way I am. It's what I do. I leave while things are still good, before sweet turns sour and good goes bad. If I have any virtue at all, it's in not pretending otherwise.''

"It doesn't have to be that way,'' Dani whispered. How could she make him believe that?

His voice changed then, going cooler, more professional, less intimate. "I just wanted you to understand now that it's over. I want to make sure you know why.''

"For the sake of your own conscience?''

He didn't answer. He was going to hang up.

"Wait! I still want my resort.'' She didn't, she realized. She didn't care about the resort anymore at all. But it was all she had left to hold him with.

Wine and dine him then jump his bones. She got back on track. "Help me,'' she said quickly.

He sounded startled. "How?''

"You said my fight is with Stan now. I want to invite him to our Los Angeles resort on Friday night—and, of course, a guest. We can fly down and have dinner, come back the next morning. I want one last chance to talk him around to my side, on my turf this time.''

"Stan unloaded all his land—to me and to you.''

"But Stan holds the injunction. That's what you just told me.''

He seemed to think about that. "You don't need me to try to get him to lift it. He's already blocked my efforts.''

She was getting desperate. "You could try to talk him around to my side, as well. Two against one."

"You want me to *collaborate* with you? Isn't it enough that I've given up?"

Dani closed her eyes helplessly. "All right, then consider it a reward for your efforts so far. I have my best chef in L.A."

He didn't answer. Then, finally, he cleared his throat. "I'll let you know."

It was the best she was going to get right now, Dani realized. She let her breath out on an unsteady sigh. When he said goodbye, she hung up and covered her face with her hands.

A million-plus dollars and all her plans and lists later, all she could do was wait.

Dani called the senator on Tuesday. He accepted her invitation graciously and immediately, which told her that he was as eager to find an easy way out of this dilemma as she had been a month ago. Then again, her chef at the Los Angeles resort really was renowned. It was possible Stan just wanted the meal she was offering.

By Thursday, Maxwell still hadn't called. Dani hugged herself and paced her office, wondering if there wasn't something else she should do. Nothing came to mind that wouldn't be embarrassing or illegal, though the idea of kidnapping him had some merit.

It wouldn't be a wasted trip, she assured herself, even if he didn't join them. She could meet with her people in the south and she would accomplish something while she was there. And who knew? Maybe she could actually talk Stan Roberson into sense where that injunction was concerned.

If Maxwell didn't join them, if he didn't give her this

last-ditch chance, she thought he might break her heart after all—and she'd have a lot less to show for it.

Now that she had an understanding of his reluctance, it made the situation even worse. He thought that nothing lasted forever. And it seemed as if he thought she was a forever kind of woman. Temper sizzled inside her. All her life men had been deciding for her what she needed, what was best. Her father had determined that she couldn't be a part of his world, and he had stashed her in motels. Richard had determined that the business should be her baby. And now Maxwell had decided that she was above a little short-term lust.

Damn it, didn't she have the right to decide that for herself?

Her telephone rang. Dani leaned across her desk and grabbed it. "Yes?"

"It's Nicole in L.A.," Angelique said. "She wants to confirm those three suites for tomorrow night."

She owned the damned place, didn't she? She could certainly reserve an extra suite she might not need if she wanted to! Of course, if everything went according to plan, she and Maxwell would only be needing one.

If he joined them, if he called…

"Yes," she said quickly. "Confirm them."

Dani hung up and started pacing again. Waiting.

"Why not?" Stan asked. "Why won't you come along?"

"You know damned well why," Max growled. There were no doubt a few bears startled out of hibernation who were in a better mood than he was at the moment, and both men knew it.

Still, Stan had the temerity to wave a hand negligently. They were having a quick lunch at his desk.

"Enjoy the evening," he suggested. "Enjoy the woman. Why does it have to be more complicated than that?"

"Because she has *designs* on me."

"No, Max. You have designs on her. And finally, for once in your life, she's someone who matters so much she scares the hell out of you."

Max's heart seized. "I don't want to hurt her," he said stubbornly. "It's better to let her down right here, right now."

"Are we back to that business about her looking at you?"

"For a long time. Damn it, it wasn't just a look. It was a *look*. It stuck in my mind and it made me crazy." That, he thought, and the red lace and the NASCAR cap and the kisses.

"Ah."

"What does that mean? Ah?" Max demanded.

"You kissed her, didn't you?" Stan asked, as though reading his mind.

Maxwell nearly dropped his iced tea. "Where did you get that from?"

"From the stuck-in-my-mind-and-crazy part. I've been there, pal, remember? I'm getting married in November."

"November? You never said you were doing it in November."

"I'm telling you now. November twenty-sixth. Mark it on your calendar. Now back to you—what's it going to be? We're supposed to meet her at the airport in two hours. Are you coming along or are you going to be stubborn?"

"I'm not going. I can't let her do what she thinks she wants to do."

"It's possible that she just has business on her mind, you know."

"Ha." The sound was flat, a bark.

"There's nothing wrong with your ego," Stan noted. "Just your mind."

"There's nothing wrong with my mind, either."

Stan shook his head. "Self-delusion is never healthy."

"How am I deluding myself?" Max scowled.

"You're telling yourself that you're sparing her, when what you're really doing is running for your life. Max—" Stan paused "—how long are you going to let our past dictate your future? Just because nothing ever lasted for you doesn't mean it never will."

Max's eyes narrowed. "Hey, you were there in those homes right along with me. You saw how we got shuffled along from home to home, and all because our own *families* couldn't bother sticking with us."

Stan crumpled his napkin and dropped it in the trash can beneath his desk. "And now you're convinced that no one else will, either. And you're not going to let go of your heart just in case you're right. That's your choice, but I feel sorry for you."

Max leaned back and stared at his friend. They'd come through their injunction battle—all caused by a woman—and had shaken hands at the end of it. Now, once again, they were on shaky ground. It sounded a lot like Stan was criticizing him.

Max watched him as he went to the closet in his office and took out his suit jacket. "Are you telling me," he asked slowly, "that you're not the least bit nervous about walking down the aisle in November?"

"I'm terrified. But I'm more scared of living without her." Stan stopped with his hand on the doorknob. "You know, if you really don't want to go, maybe Joe Lanigan would want to take your place. I mean, it seems somewhat awkward for Marcy and I both to go and put Danielle Harrington without an...I don't know, an escort, I guess one would say. It just seems insensitive to me.''

"Then leave Marcy home.''

"Ah, but she's so excited about the trip.''

"Who the hell is Joe Lanigan, anyway?'' Max snarled.

"Councilman, District Two. Newly divorced.''

"That ought to tell him something.''

"Well, it didn't. He's not an idiot.''

Max reared to his feet.

"Then again,'' Stan said quickly, "I can't just invite someone else without checking with her first—Danielle Harrington, that is. Do you happen to know her number offhand? Never mind. I can get it.''

Stan left—fast. Which was just as well, Max thought, because he'd just realized both his fists were clenched and he was feeling violent.

He wasn't going to do it.

Dani stood beneath the wing of the Gulfstream jet that the corporation leased. She wondered if she had even once stopped hugging herself since Tuesday. There was a chill in her bones that she couldn't quite shake loose.

They were set to take off in fifteen minutes. And Maxwell hadn't called.

She waited until the shiver that took her was more from the cool coastal air than anything she was feeling inside, then she went slowly up the steps to the aircraft door. It was elegantly appointed in rich, hunter-green leather and brass trim. It left her cold.

An earnest young man met her there, one of the stewards. "Ms. Harrington, can I get you anything before we take off?"

Yes, she thought. He's about six feet tall with dark hair and blue eyes. And he's a very good fighter who cares about small defenseless things like birds. He knows what it is to be truly alone.

"Papaya juice," she said quietly. "That would be fine."

She sat to wait for the senator and his fiancée. Just as the steward brought her glass and she took a sip, she heard the sound of footsteps outside on the metal steps. A lot of footsteps.

Her heart seized. Dani stood quickly and pivoted to face the door.

The senator came first, looking casual and yet somehow debonair in a sweater and slacks. His girlfriend was a very pretty, chic blonde. And there, behind them, was Maxwell.

Her breath left her. He stopped in the door and looked around until his gaze found hers. Her heart lifted. She smiled and wondered if it shook. He finally nodded.

"Still have room for one more?"

Chapter Twelve

Max was already doubting his sanity when the flight took off.

He'd allowed himself to be goaded by Stan—which was all this was—and as far as motivation was concerned, he knew it was purely stupid. He hadn't changed his mind about Dani. He wasn't a cruel man. He wouldn't contribute to her...to her designs.

He was here just on the off chance that Joe Lanigan might be inclined to take his place. But that was wrong, too.

He was here to help her sway Stan. To give her the one thing she really needed. The resort.

That explanation felt the most comfortable, and Max tried to relax.

Dani glanced over at the other side of the plane. The senator and his girlfriend—her name was Marcy—had their heads together, laughing together and whispering like children. They were clearly so happy together that it made her breath hitch. It also seemed like a deliberate plan on Stan Roberson's part to leave her and Maxwell alone.

But as they strapped in and talked idly, she felt like an imposter. For all intents and purposes, Maxwell was her date for this little excursion. But he didn't tilt his head toward hers the way Stan did toward Marcy. He didn't want to be here. It was written all over his face, stamped on his posture.

Why *had* he joined them then?

Her knuckles whitened over her armrests and she held her breath until they were airborne. Max noticed. "Hey, you pay the pilot. You have no one to blame but yourself if we go down."

She closed her eyes. "Don't say that." When she looked at him again, his expression was curious.

"You're really afraid of flying."

"I'm afraid of anything where I'm not in control."

"That's why you don't have a driver. Why you zip around all over town in that little green car by yourself. And here I thought it was just the sun on your face and the feeling of the wind in your hair."

He understood, she realized, and that only made their time together more poignant. If this didn't work and they landed in northern California again tomorrow and he walked away from her once and for all, she didn't know how she'd handle it. So few people in her life had bothered to take the time to look inside her.

"It's both," she said quietly. "When I'm in my car, being alone is just a matter of being free." The pilot turned the seat belt light out and she sighed. "I didn't think you were going to join us."

"You're changing the subject."

"Am I?"

"When was the last time you had fun, the last time you felt free instead of alone?"

"When I was driving back from your office last week and I decided to buy that other land."

"That made you happy?"

"The thought of besting you? Oh, yes."

She grinned. He grinned back.

"It's your turn now," she said.

"I don't remember agreeing to exchange questions this time."

"Chicken."

He raised a brow at her. "What was yours again?"

"I'll make it easy on you and turn yours right back your way. When was the last time you were happy?"

"Watching you pick your way barefoot through the dunes the other night."

The answer came quickly enough to startle her. And she knew from his expression that it had caught him off guard, as well.

"When I was arriving or when I was leaving?" she asked cautiously. She had waited a long time that night for his headlights to come on . When they hadn't, she'd left the beach—and him—behind.

"Arriving. I wasn't glad to see you go."

She smiled, a quick look that tickled her mouth, then she looked out the window again and fell quiet. Maxwell thought again that he was playing Russian roulette here. She sat across from him in a simple black dress that stopped several inches shy of her knees. She crossed one leg over the other in that way she had. This time his mouth didn't go dry. He just yearned.

He wished he were a different man, one with less of a conscience. Then he heard Stan's voice again. *You're not sparing her. You're running for your life.*

She sighed, her breasts rising and falling with the breath, and Max realized that he really *was* scared to death. She called to him in a deep, elemental way; she had from the start. Stan was right. Yes, maybe he could stay. And maybe, once the novelty wore off, she would go…just like everyone else had gone.

And that would kill him this time…because he was in love with her.

"What?" He realized that Dani had said something to him. His heart was pistoning.

"The suite that Richard and I always used in Los Angeles has a balcony," she repeated. "We'll dine there. It overlooks the sea but it should be somewhat warmer there than in Gold Beach. I think it will be pleasant."

He wasn't Richard Harrington, Maxwell thought frantically. He wasn't dignified, as mature as fine red wine. *That* was the kind of man she stayed with. He was just a down-to-earth guy, tooling around the beach in a Jeep.

He'd fallen in love with her.

"Does it bother you staying there now that he's gone?" he heard himself ask, his voice raw. "In that room?"

She gave him a smile that could only be described as sad. "Ah, well, we rarely stayed there together."

Max raised a brow and waited.

"Richard always felt it was better to divide—our own resources that is—and conquer. We didn't generally travel together. One of us usually stayed behind to oversee things at corporate headquarters."

He was beginning to get a picture, Max thought. And this might be the most terrifying thing of all. Harrington had been her mentor, and probably her best friend. He'd been her partner in many senses of the word. But Max wasn't sure he'd been her lover, not in the fully passionate sense of the word. He remembered kissing her again. There were unplumbed depths inside her, fault lines just waiting for the right vibration so they could open and part and everything she was could come tumbling out...in some lucky man's arms.

He couldn't be that man. He didn't dare.

Max undid his seat belt and got to his feet quickly. "Stan."

His friend looked over at him, startled.

"I'll keep Marcy company," he continued. "Why don't you and Danielle start trying to negotiate some kind of compromise on Gold Beach once and for all?"

Danielle? He was back to calling her *Danielle?* Dani watched him join the senator's girlfriend and her heart sank.

It was going to be a very long night.

By the time dinner was served on the spacious balcony of her room, Dani was no closer to a settlement with the senator than she had been four weeks ago. And she couldn't even pretend to care.

She had, indeed, pulled out all the stops. They'd had an appetizer of escargot in puff pastry, her chef's speciality. There were veal medallions with asparagus and mushrooms in a white wine sauce. She'd served the finest vintage wine. Flickering candles were set deep in glass so the errant breeze wouldn't blow them out. There was a violinist for soft, accompanying mood music.

As she sipped her coffee after dinner, her hands shook. There was, after all, nothing left to do but attempt to...how had Angelique put it? Jump Maxwell's bones.

Her heart quailed. It wasn't her style. She didn't even know where to start. She needed help.

"Vincent," she said quickly to their waiter. He hurried from the shadows to their table. "Could you please bring us some cognac?"

"My pleasure, ma'am."

He was gone and back in a flash, with four snifters. Dani lifted hers and drank deeply. Okay, she could do this. She *could.* "Maxwell."

"Hmm?" He had been speaking to Marcy, but he looked at her quickly.

"Let's dance."

He looked around. "Where?"

As if on cue, the violinist moved forward to serenade them. "Here," she said. "Right here."

Stan Roberson got to his feet. "Danielle, dinner was delightful. I thank you for your charming hospitality. But my bride-to-be and I would like to retire."

Dani looked his way. He *had* been giving them a wide berth all night, just as she'd suspected. And now he was going to leave them alone. *Bless him.*

"Of course." She stood and offered him her hand. "Your room should have everything you need. But if anything's lacking, please just call Cynthia downstairs. You'll find her extension number on your nightstand."

Marcy rose as well. "I'm sure everything will be perfect. Thank you."

Dani watched them go, then she looked at Maxwell. He was still seated.

"Dance?" he echoed.

She refused to acknowledge that his expression looked like that of a deer caught in headlights. She wrung her hands before she knew she was doing it, then she dropped them quickly to her sides. "Please. I love to dance."

"As much as you love baseball?"

"More."

How was he supposed to say no when she whispered that last little word? Especially since he didn't want to say no. Maxwell found himself rising from his chair, holding his arms out to her.

She came into them like a dream slipping across his mind in the darkest hours of the night. Gliding there, filling what had only been air and emptiness just a moment before. Fitting there as though she belonged to him.

"Ah," she said against his shoulder. That sea mist scent, light but clinging, drifted up from her hair.

"Dani."

"Yes?" She tilted her face up to look at him. And her eyes said, *make this last forever.*

His heart staggered. She began moving to the music, smoothly and with grace, but he could feel the tension in her muscles under his palms as he coasted his hands along her back.

"Dani, don't," he said hoarsely.

"Don't dance?"

"Don't make me want you."

"Ah, a fate worse than death." But he felt her stiffen in his arms even more.

"I've got to make you understand this. You're a woman who ought to be up to her elbows in cookie dough with three kids gathered around her. You're the kind who tilts her face up for a kiss hello when her husband comes home from work. You ought to be in a house somewhere with toys in the yard and a swing set in the back, and flowers that you planted yourself all up and down the drive. I can't give you any of that." *But he didn't want anyone else to give it to her, either.*

He realized belatedly that with every word he spoke, she trembled a little more.

"I'm not any of those things," she breathed.

"No." His mouth was too damned close to hers. "But you should be."

Suddenly she was out of his arms, and the transformation staggered him. She whipped back and raked her hands through her hair. In the moonlight her eyes were on fire. Anger sang through her body like a bow vibrating with tension just a moment before the arrow was loosed.

She was furious. And she was magnificent.

"How *dare* you." Her words hummed with the force of her emotion. "How dare you presume to know what's best for me!" The hell of it was, she thought, every word he'd spoken had made her ache more. They'd made her *want* all those things he'd spoken of.

But not with any man. With him.

She had fallen in love with him. And that infuriated her even more.

She marched toward him and stabbed a finger against his chest. "I don't have three kids, and I make hotels instead of cookies." She poked him again. "Damn you, nobody kisses me when he comes home at night! The gardener takes care of the stupid flowers! All I ever wanted from you was this!" Her temper gave her courage. She leaned into him and kissed him again...hard.

She meant it to be hard. There was certainly heat inside her and need and greed...for once to just take something for herself, something *she* wanted, something no one else had dictated for her. And maybe because she wanted to brand him with what he would be missing when he left this time for good.

She sealed her mouth to his and then it happened. His mouth softened, going tender. And that made the stars spin over her head and the night whirl about her. Her hands found his shoulders and she hung on.

"I'll hurt you," he said against her mouth.

She caught her breath—and this time she pushed him away. "I think you already have."

He swore, a colorful word that she hadn't heard since her days of touring with her father. Then he stepped around her and went back inside. Too late, far too late, she reached a single hand out to stop him. But her fingers found air and she let her hand fall back to her side. A cry caught in her throat.

Dani followed a long minute later. Everything inside her still hummed, still hurt. He was gone. The suite was vacant. She wandered, listening to the silence, so much deeper than ever before when she had been here alone. She went back to the balcony and looked around dazedly.

At some point the waiter and the violinist had left also. She had the place to herself.

She sat down at the table and cried.

Dani woke early the next morning, her nerves still feeling raw, her head heavy and dense as though someone had filled it with soggy cotton. She rolled onto her back...and felt like crying all over again.

Maxwell was no different from any other man she'd known...except he didn't even want the little pieces of her that her father and Richard had taken. He didn't want anything from her at all. She squeezed her eyes shut. Trust her—with her track record—to fall in love with the one man in the world who had enough integrity to worry about the long term.

Her father had tucked her away on the road, but sometimes they had gone home and he'd taken her to the beach. Richard had loved her—she knew that—but in so many ways he, too, had stood back and pulled her strings like a marionette.

She wanted to feel. She wanted the fire. She wanted to love and be loved. But somehow, instead, on yet another morning, she was waking up cold and alone.

She groaned and sat up, putting her feet to the floor. Somehow she was going to have to leave this room and face him, even though she'd pulled out all the stops and she had flopped on her face. She'd flopped miserably.

She ordered coffee to be sent to her room and she took a long time showering. She stalled as much as she was able, checking her lipstick three times. At a quarter to eight, there was nothing else she could do but go downstairs.

She checked in at the desk first, out of habit. She was, above all else, a businesswoman. Nicole, the day shift manager, hadn't arrived yet, but Cynthia, who oversaw the guests' needs at night, was still there.

"Oh, Ms. Harrington, how did it go last evening?"

Dani winced. *Horrible.* But, of course, that was no fault of her staff. "Everything was done to perfection. Thank you."

"I'll pass it on to Nicole and I'm sure she'll tell Chef."

"You do that." Dani started to turn away.

"I asked because one of your guests left this for you. I was afraid there was a problem."

Dani turned back to the woman. Cynthia was holding out a small, folded piece of paper. And just like that, Dani knew.

He hadn't even said goodbye, at least not to her face.

"How did he leave?" she asked woodenly. "We flew down in the jet."

"He asked me to arrange for a rental car. I did. I hope that was okay. Of course I had the company bill the resort."

"What time?" Dani whispered.

"At just about six o'clock."

Dani nodded. "Thank you."

She didn't open the note until she reached the dining room. The senator and his fiancé had not arrived downstairs yet. Dani said a prayer of thanks for small miracles. She took a table by herself and opened the note.

"Business called me back early this morning. I thank you for your hospitality. I sincerely hope you and Stan can work something out. Best wishes, Maxwell."

So polite. So proper.

So cold.

A cry caught in her throat. Dani swallowed it back ruthlessly and just in time. She looked up to see Stan and Marcy approach her table.

Stan looked around at the empty seats. "Where's Max?"

Dani cleared her throat carefully. "Ah, business called him back north early this morning. Please, sit down. Let's have breakfast and officially determine that we haven't solved our dilemma and we aren't likely to."

She watched them sit and she talked on, smoothly, seamlessly, charmingly. She was her father's daughter, Richard's protégée, after all. It was only in the deepest parts of her mind that she acknowledged an awful truth, and it never showed on her face.

For the first time in her life, she was without hope.

Chapter Thirteen

As many times as she'd thought about selling Richard's house, and as deeply as Maxwell's words about having her own gardens had cut her, Dani still found a numbing relief in getting home.

Under overcast skies that looked more or less the way her heart felt, she picked her car up in the airport parking lot. She drove back to Gold Beach with the top down, anyway. There was no sun on her face, but the wind felt good against her flushed cheeks. She left the BMW in front of the steps, not bothering to slip it into the garage. What was the sense of being rich without a loyal employee to come running for it before it could rain?

She stepped into the huge marble entry and dropped her jacket over the newel post. Immediately, Mrs. Dunley appeared to pluck it up again.

"Ms. Harrington?" the housekeeper asked tentatively at the look on her face. "Are you all right?"

"I'm fine." Dani covered her face with her hands briefly and scrubbed her cheeks. Then she let her head fall back and she took a deep breath. Fortified again, she set off for Richard's study.

She wanted scotch.

This was definitely a scotch occasion. She'd made an idiot of herself, and somehow she had managed to do it in front of a state senator and his very attractive girl-friend. She snagged a bottle from the bar and lifted it to her husband's memory in a toast.

"At least you never ran from me like I was a leper, and for that I am grateful," she murmured. Then she poured herself a stiff shot and tossed it back.

It ran like a stream of fire down her throat, and when it landed, it shot little sparks all through the rest of her system. Dani shivered from something a whole lot more manageable than Maxwell Padgett. She would drink more of this, she decided. Maybe she would even get drunk. She had never done that before in her life, but, after all, there was no man left to tell her that it wasn't her style.

She took the bottle upstairs to her bedroom and kept it close while she showered and changed into a warm, comfortable robe. She left a message on her voice mail at the office saying she wouldn't be in this afternoon after all. She almost always showed up at some point on Saturdays, and when she didn't, she knew someone would check the messages. She added a quick addendum in case it was Angelique who collected them. She didn't want to be disturbed at home.

Finally she curled up on her window seat with the bottle in one hand and her glass in the other. This win-dow faced the sea. Somewhere way out there, at the bottom of the hills, plovers nested.

She was still mortified by what had happened in L.A. But after another drink, one she sipped this time, something started to twitch inside her. It was sharp and edgy…and she liked it.

She was *mad* again. Madder than she had been when Max had murmured inane, self-serving platitudes about hurting her. She was mad at him…and at herself. She was mad at everyone in her nice, tidy, rich world.

It was time for some changes, she decided suddenly.

For the first time in her life, she had thrown herself at a man—*thrown* herself at him. And he had walked away from her. Yes, it was humiliating. And yes, his rationale was insulting. But…she had learned something from it, she realized.

He *had* been attracted to her. He just wasn't willing to do anything about it. So she had learned that red lace was good.

She had discovered that having money to throw around gave her a certain kick.

She had discovered that baseball stadiums were awesome places.

She now knew that cooking was best left to the housekeepers of the world, and…she was damned if she was ever going to go back to toeing the line ever again.

Where had it gotten her? she thought, pouring more scotch. The best thing that could be said about her experience with Maxwell was that she had *felt* for a little while. For moments, for hours, she'd been alive. He, too, had tried to dictate what she wanted, what she needed. But somewhere in the process she'd discovered that there was a Dani hiding inside Danielle.

And she liked her.

Her board members might have thought that she'd lost her mind this past month, but no one had ousted her yet, had they? No! And they wouldn't. Because even in her wildest moments, they knew she made them money. She *always* made them money. They would live with her eccentricities. And if they didn't?

Well then, she'd learned something else, as well. She'd learned that that corporation couldn't make her shiver inside. It couldn't make her yearn.

She stood carefully from the window seat and made her way across the room. She picked up the telephone, then she punched in the home number of her head accountant.

"Paul," she said when he answered. "It's Dani Harrington."

"Dan—oh." He sounded discomfitted by her casual announcement.

"I have a small favor to ask, but it needs to be done today. I'm going to have to ask you to go into the office. You'll be compensated for it, I promise."

"What's that, Ms. Harrington?"

"I want to transfer ownership of the Gold Beach lots I own to that plover fund I set up last month, along with the one they already have."

"You *what?*"

"It has to be done today." Because, she thought, she was making a fresh start. And there was no time like the present.

"Ms. Harrington, that's a million-three worth of land. And then some."

"Paul, I purchased it. I know that."

"The one lot belongs to the corporation."

"And I am the CEO."

"That's true, but—"

"Transfer it, Paul. We'll build the new resort in the peaks." She hung up on him, then she made a few more phone calls. By the time she was done, she had reassigned the architect, the building crews and assorted others to the peaks property. And she knew, when she hung up, that she had won something far more precious than her plover war with Maxwell Padgett.

She'd won control over her world, without fear of what others thought, that they would abandon her if she didn't play by their rules. So what if they did? She could not feel any more isolated than she did now.

Dani poured one more glass of scotch. She had set herself free. She was not going to be beholden to anyone anymore, not her father's memory or the responsibilities that Richard had chained her to. She was going to start making her own decisions and living for herself.

She had never felt better, she realized. And besides, she had never wanted to disenfranchise all those birds.

She finally put her still-full glass carefully on the night table. Then she flopped down on the bed and pulled the comforter up over her. She slept like she hadn't done in ages.

The only person in Maxwell's office who wasn't shouting or otherwise poleaxed was Max himself. He leaned back in his chair, frowning. In some measure he'd felt this coming.

Stan was exuberant. He was still dressed in his break-fast-in-Los-Angeles finest, peach-colored slacks and a white patterned sweater. He'd come to the coalition office as soon as Max had called him.

"You dog," he hooted. "You had this up your sleeve all along. What did you say to her last night?"

Max shook his head. "I didn't do this." It would be easy to assume that she was just trying another tactic to...well, to hook him, but he knew in his gut that that wasn't it.

She was washing her hands of the whole situation.

Something bloomed in his chest, filling it, and it was painful. He'd lost her. He'd done everything his conscience had demanded and he was alone as he'd meant to be, as he should be. And in that moment he discovered there was something worse than taking a chance with someone else's heart.

How had Stan put it? *I'm more afraid of living without her.*

He hadn't understood then, Max thought. He knew emptiness, but this echo wasn't like anything he had ever met before.

"That is one rich lady," Roger murmured. "She really did this? That's over a million dollars worth of land."

"Well, it's tax deductible," someone pointed out.

"The transfer went through an hour ago," Max muttered.

"I still don't understand why," Roger fretted.

But Max knew the answer to that. This act, this one single act, was the real Dani. She hadn't known a damned thing about baseball and he wasn't in a hurry to try out her cooking. Nor was she—or had she ever been—cutthroat enough to plow under plover nests in the name of commerce. All she'd been doing with that beach land was chasing a memory. And a woman who held on that tightly, that desperately, to a man who had shunted her aside and stuck her in hotel rooms would not hurt birds.

So this, he thought, was real. He picked up the phone and called her office while everyone else in the room talked and slapped high-fives.

"Ms. Harrington is not in, sir," came a tired, Saturday-only-employee kind of voice. "Would you like her secretary's voice mail?"

Max started to say no, then he reconsidered. When the beep came, he said, "This message is for Dani Harrington. It's Max Padgett. I need to speak with her as soon as possible." He disconnected.

She wouldn't get the message until Monday. He was sure of it. He couldn't wait that long. He stood and shrugged into his jacket.

"Where are you going?" Stan asked, surprised.

"To find her."

Something flared in his best friend's eyes. "How's your breathing these days?"

"Not good. Not good at all." He'd thrown away the only real, honest thing that had ever happened to him...maybe the only thing that would last.

He left the office and got into his Jeep. He tried briefly—fruitlessly—to ease all the blame off himself. Was it his fault, really? She'd given him as many different personas as he had hairs on his head! How was he supposed to have known that underneath all that was a woman strong enough to run a multimillion-dollar corporation at the same time she ached for someone to hold her?

Because she'd risked that corporation—throwing money all over the place and jeopardizing her reputation—just for a piece of his time.

He still had nothing to give her, Max thought as he turned the Jeep inland. But she had everything to give him. And he'd known it from the first time he'd laid eyes on her, that night in her office when she had crossed her legs gently and had flinched when he'd mentioned that she was alone. He'd known and he'd run...like a fool. Now he would dig down to the bottom of his soul to find something she could hold on to, also.

And he would stay.

The big red-brick fortress of her home looked silent and forbidding when he pulled up in the drive. It gave him a bad feeling. He left the Jeep and went to the door to lift the brass knocker. This time it was answered almost immediately by a woman with tight gray curls. She wore black, all black, from her hose and her shoes up to her starched, neat dress.

"We don't take solicitors," she said stiffly.

"I'm Max Padgett. I'm not selling anything. I came to see Ms. Harrington."

"I'm sorry, sir. She's not available. Would you like to leave a message? I'll have her get back to you at a more convenient time."

Ouch. "Ask her to call me. Tell her I need to talk to her. Wait." She wouldn't have his home number, he thought, and Monday was still feeling like a long way away. He took a scrap of paper from his pocket and a pen and scribbled it down. "Here's my address as well. Tell her that if she wants to, she can just barge in unannounced."

He handed it over to the woman. She looked down at it and frowned.

Max turned silently and went back to his Jeep. He heard the door swoosh and click shut behind him. It sounded very final.

"What do you think?" On Thursday evening, Dani stepped out of the dressing room of the beach's finest local clothing store. She wore a short red dress with long sleeves, elegant and utterly provocative with a demure slit up one side.

"I think," Angelique said, "that you're having a nervous breakdown."

"You're the one who told me to ditch the suits." Dani

spun in front of the mirror and kept her chin high, but something in her heart cracked a little when she thought that it had been because of Maxwell that she'd gotten that advice. It seemed like a lifetime ago now.

She hadn't spoken to him, though she knew he'd been trying to reach her. He'd left messages at the office and with Mrs. Dunley, but Dani couldn't bear even another one of his apologies. And she had made a vow to herself before the Los Angeles trip. If she failed, she would walk away.

There was just no sense in clinging to him any longer.

"That was at the beginning of all this," Angelique muttered. "The advice about the suits was just to get things off the ground."

"So now we're at the end of it," Dani said.

"The suits...well, suited you."

"No. They suited the woman who was married to Richard."

"*You* were married to Richard."

Dani went still at that. It was a truth as deep as her heart. And yet, Richard was the cliff she was jumping off. She was finally jumping, for the first time in her life.

Angelique shrugged. "Oh, what the hell. Buy it. The red looks great with your hair. I still don't know what you're trying to prove, but go for it. Just take it slow."

Dani whirled on her. "I've taken it slow for thirty-six years. And you know where it's gotten me? Childless and without a garden to call my own."

"Huh?" Angelique looked confused.

Dani turned her back on her and looked for the sales-girl. "I'll take this dress and those black Capri slacks also. With that funny little top."

"A million-three on land, a thousand and a half

here…I hope you know what you're doing,'' Angelique muttered.

"I'm finally spending some of that damned money,'' Dani said. Her heart was breaking though. Because none of this, not selling the land or all these clothes, *nothing* made her feel the way she had felt when she'd looked into Maxwell's eyes.

She thought about asking Angelique about generally how long it might take to get over a man. Then she decided that she probably didn't want to know.

When his telephone hadn't rung by Friday—not with her voice on the other end of the line, at least—Maxwell knew what he had to do. It was sneaky. It was underhanded. It was a ploy. But who better to perpetrate it on than the baseball-fan-turned-Betty-Crocker?

She'd hadn't sailed into his office. She hadn't arrived at his town house door. She'd shut him out. So he put Stan's people on the problem. He'd kept tabs on what she was up to with the new resort. What good was it to front one of the heaviest lobbies in the country if not to get the attention of a certain CEO?

On Friday morning he made two telephone calls and got what he wanted. By midafternoon, he was on his way up to the peaks.

The wind was fierce here, Dani thought, and it was something that worried her. She stood at the new site with her architect, her engineer and the surveyors, and she felt a headache bloom behind her eyes. What she had done in scotch-induced indignation last week still seemed right emotionally. But as the CEO of Harrington Resorts and Enterprises, Ltd., she had a problem on her hands where these gusts were concerned.

"Windbreaks,'' she said, scraping the hair back from

her face and holding it. "There's got to be such a thing."

"Anything substantial enough to do any good would break the view," said her architect.

"The wind here is mostly east-northeast," one of the surveyors said. "We could put up a stand of timber over there and it would solve the problem." He pointed in a diagonal direction from the sea.

The idea had some merit, Dani thought, but then her mind emptied. She looked up and saw Maxwell's Jeep stop on a far dirt road.

There was nothing so fine as a curb here at this site. She was starting from scratch. She stared at the vehicle, telling herself that from this distance, she could be mistaken. Then a man emerged from the passenger side door of his vehicle, the one who had served her with injunction papers a month ago. *It was the court officer.* And then Maxwell left the Jeep, as well, and joined him. She'd know the way he moved anywhere.

Dani's headache exploded. Her temper threw off fireworks. She bore down on them as they approached her. "What?" she demanded. "What now?"

"I'm sorry, ma'am." The court official handed papers over to her. Dani reared back from them.

"This time I won't take them." She turned blazing eyes on Max. "There's not a plover within fifteen miles of here!"

"Worms," Max said complacently.

"*Worms?* What worms?"

"Semipalmated earthworms."

She felt her gaze drawn to his hands again. And she *still* wondered what they would feel like on her skin. She still didn't know. "Worms come in that variety, too?" she asked shortly.

"Yes. And you're destroying all their reproductive tendencies."

"I'm *what?*" Then she looked at him. And something in his eyes made her heart stop. Hope filled all the emptiness inside her all over again.

It was dangerous, it was crazy, to risk wanting him again, and she held her breath.

"They're on the endangered species list?" she asked carefully.

"Not yet. But there are only six trillion of them left on earth. I feel compelled to start somewhere."

She felt laughter work up from her chest, a giddy, full feeling. "You won't miss the million or so you'll lose here."

"Ah, but we will. Someday."

"I'll begin a Coalition for Gardeners Everywhere. We feel strongly that earthworms must go."

"And will you start with a garden of your own?"

He watched her levelly. Dani felt her heart squeeze.

She had also put Richard's elegant and far-too-huge home up for sale this week. She was going to buy something smaller. Something with a lawn. And a garden. She cleared her throat. She would definitely have a garden. She shrugged. "A woman does what a woman has to do."

The court man with the papers backed off. Dani never noticed. Maxwell held a hand out to her.

"Don't do this to me," he said, capturing hers.

"Don't make you want me?"

"Don't shut me out."

Her heart shook again. He meant it. She could see it in his eyes…and above all, he was honest. But she had to be sure. "I never did that. It was the other way around."

"We're all entitled to our mistakes."

"Mistakes?" Dani cleared her throat. "So...are you telling me that your plovers don't need that beach after all?" Then she grinned. She realized she was toying with him—*her*...as naturally and easily as though she had been flirting all of her life.

"I don't know what they need," Max said seriously. "I just know I need you."

She felt everything inside her crack and splinter. Everything that had held her together for days. She felt shaky. Suddenly she felt a little scared. She cleared her throat. "I should probably tell you...you never got the real me."

"Yes. I think I did."

"You don't understand. I might come to love baseball but that's a very small ball to get so worked up about. And I really can't cook."

"Surprise, surprise." His eyes held hers. His lips crooked up in a smile. "I dare you to deny that you're crazy as a loon."

"Me?" She wasn't quite sure how to take that.

"Giving away a million three hundred thousand dollars' worth of land."

"Oh. That. I'm rich."

"Five hundred thousand was corporate money."

"They'll live with it."

"You gave it to my cause."

Her heart was thudding. "I gave it to my past."

That he didn't expect. Max frowned.

"I got tired of everything that held me to a life—to a woman—who never made her own choices," Dani explained. "So I made my own, even if it was obscenely expensive."

He nodded. "Your heart is strong. I'm counting on that."

Strong? It quaked inside her.

"Dani, I'm willing to believe that *we* can last. I'm willing to try it."

Her heart exploded. "What are you saying?"

"If you promise me you won't cook or spend my money as wildly as you spend yours, I want you in my life. I need you. I love you. Marry me."

Her heart went still. Then she laughed while tears gathered in her eyes. She launched herself toward him, into his arms. "I love you, too."

And as she stood in the circle of his love, she realized she had finally won her man.

Epilogue

Dani almost missed the arrival of the swing set because she was up to her elbows in cookie dough.

The cookie dough was somewhat the worse for the wear with the fingers of several children probing eagerly into it. The little ones were jammed between Dani and the counter, four of them ranging in age from three to eleven. The three-year-old was getting beaten in the shuffle.

"Sam, lift Alyssa so she can get a swipe," Dani chided.

The eleven-year-old grumbled and complained but he lifted the toddler. He was coming along, Dani thought, giving more and more of himself each day. As Max said, it was all a matter of trust, of believing he would be here with them forever.

And he would. They had adopted him out of the system.

The situation with Alyssa was too soon to call yet— her mother was in rehab, and they were hopeful she would recover enough to take her child home. Eight-year-old Lindsey and ten-year-old Thomas had been abandoned, not unlike Max had. The staggering amount of red tape required to make them their own hadn't quite gone through yet. But in the meantime they were all safe and secure, well fed and well loved, in the Padgett home.

It certainly beat throwing money at beach land and birds, Dani thought, grinning.

"What's this?" Thomas asked, snagging her attention.

She plucked a chocolate chip from the dough for herself and looked toward the window where he was standing. "What's what?"

"Big truck," Thomas observed.

With a little more time and effort, she thought, they might even get Thomas to talk past monosyllables. She went to the window and stood behind him. Then her jaw dropped. "I have no idea."

"Good store," Thomas observed.

In fact, Dani thought, it was a major national toy store. *What had Max done now?*

As if to answer her question, the front door slammed at the other end of Richard Harrington's cavernous house. Dani smiled again in anticipation. She wiped her hands on a towel and looked around at the children. It had turned out that there was more than one use for these huge, empty rooms, so she had taken it off the market again when she and Max had gotten married. With all the space here, she thought, they could adopt half the kids in the system and their only real problem would be misplacing one or two of them occasionally in all the hidden nooks and crannies.

She started the long trek up the center hallway to find Maxwell.

"There's a very large truck in the backyard," she said when she reached him. She tilted her face up for his kiss.

"Really? There should be two. By the way, you have cookie dough in your hair."

Dani swiped at it, then immediately forgot it. "Two? Why two?"

"One for the jungle gym and one for the hot house."

"The *what?*"

In response, he turned her back in the direction she had come from. They returned to the kitchen, and Max guided her to the window again. Now there *were* two trucks out there, the one unloading pieces of a swing set and the other from a garden center. Men were relieving that one of several glass panels.

"A hot house." Dani sighed with happiness.

"It only makes sense in a climate where the temperature gets above sixty degrees maybe three times a year."

"It only goes *below* sixty three times a year, too." But she hardly felt like arguing. She kissed him again. "Thank you."

"Just keep planting gardens in our yard." He took her into his arms.

"Always."

There was a banging sound as the kids tore outside through a servant's door tucked in one corner of the kitchen. They whooped and hollered on their way to the first truck. Dani winced and put her hands to her ears. "Are you sure you want to keep adopting?"

"Absolutely. Where's Mrs. Dunley?" he asked of the housekeeper.

"Last I saw her, she was cleaning your office."

Max grinned slowly and tugged on her hand to take

her back to the sweeping central staircase. "Good. She can watch the kids while we keep working on one of our own."

She let him lead the way to the bedroom. "You," she said, "were definitely worth the effort."

*　*　*　*　*

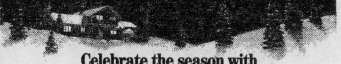

Coming in November from

SILHOUETTE *Romance*

and *New York Times* bestselling author

Kasey Michaels

BACHELOR ON THE PROWL

Colin Rafferty is a true-blue bachelor—marriage has never entered his mind. And frantic personal assistant Holly Hollis doesn't have time to think about romance. But when their friends and family get the notion that Colin and Holly would make the perfect couple...well, the bachelor isn't going to be on the prowl for long.

Don't miss this delightful spin-off to Kasey Michaels's popular novel, *Lion on the Prowl*, available from Silhouette Romance.

Available wherever Silhouette books are sold.

Silhouette®
Where love comes alive™

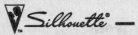